Praise for Wayne

"Of all Canadian writers, Wayne Curtis is the one I keep coming back to. He is perhaps the greatest unsung talent in the country."
– David Adams Richards

"The closeness to detail vibrates with an honesty which bears witness to lives lived humbly and poignantly. Wayne Curtis is a splendid writer."
– Alistair MacLeod

"A sensitive and insightful writer of the short story, Curtis' prose has a solid core and a rhythm that carries the reader along."
– Sinclair Ross

"A seductive storyteller wholly immersed in the world he vividly creates, Curtis reveals himself to be a lyrical and sensuous stylist."
– The Globe and Mail

"Curtis' prose is more true-to-life than most current short fiction."
– Quill and Quire

"The prose of Wayne Curtis is beautiful to read, for no detail escapes his discerning eye."
– Books in Canada

"Curtis has an eye for the telling detail, giving us the most information about a character in the fewest possible words."
– The New Brunswick Reader

River People

Wayne Curtis

Pottersfield Press, Lawrencetown Beach, Nova Scotia,
Canada

Library and Archives Canada Cataloguing in Publication

Title: River people / Wayne Curtis.
Names: Curtis, Wayne, 1943- author.
Identifiers: Canadiana (print) 20210354569 | Canadiana (ebook) 20210360801 | ISBN 9781989725757 (softcover) | ISBN 9781989725764 (PDF)
Subjects: LCGFT: Short stories.
Classification: LCC PS8555.U844 R58 2022 | DDC C813/.54—dc23

Cover image: Adobe Stock

Author photo by Stanya

Cover design: Gail LeBlanc

Pottersfield Press gratefully acknowledges the financial support of the Government of Canada for our publishing activities through the Canada Book Fund. We also acknowledge the support of the Canada Council for the Arts and the Province of Nova Scotia which has assisted us to develop and promote our creative industries for the benefit of all Nova Scotians.

Pottersfield Press
248 Leslie Road
East Lawrencetown, Nova Scotia, Canada, B2Z 1T4
Website: www.pottersfieldpress.com
To order, phone 1-800-NIMBUS9 (1-800-646-2879) www.nimbus.ns.ca

Printed in Canada

For Jennifer, Lori, and Michelle

Contents

War Bride

Long ago in my schooldays, as far back as mid-April and the Easter holidays, my sisters, mother, and I looked forward to the month of May and, among other things, our annual May picnic. This, along with our "move out" to the summer kitchen and fly-fishing for black salmon, was a tradition that Mamma brought with her from the United Kingdom, spring rituals that had been in her extended family for many generations.

In wait, from our northeastern New Brunswick farmhouse, we observed the bright morning sun that peeked over the treed horizon, a little earlier and slightly further to the east each morning. It gave the snow crust a pink sheen and started the river ice melting, ever so slightly, to leave a strip of black water along each shore. We watched as patches of bare ground beside the riverbank grew from mustaches into full-grown beards, and the amber highway turned from a mix of mud and ice into potter's clay. This froze in the nights, to thaw in the late mornings ever so slowly and by evening be moulded into deep, mud-filled ruts. The old roadstead eventually became a graded bed of packed earth, infringed with budding alder, pussy willow, and dogwood that made the scattered gravel stones pop under the fenders of our pickup trucks. Later, in the spring when the sun strengthened, a cloud of dust boiled up behind moving vehicles to drift across our greening fields. For Mamma, this had been the road into Thornton, but it would not necessarily be her way out.

My father, a third-generation Irishman, was a woodsman, farmer, and a river guide. He was happy in his world and wanted for nothing more. Having gotten out of jail at the age of thirty-one – he had been charged with getting a young woman from Spruce Landing pregnant, a secret kept from Mamma until after she arrived in Canada – he enlisted in the army where he served in England for over a year. It was there that he met and married my mother, in spite of her father having started a stop-the-wedding campaign.

When Papa and his war bride arrived in New Brunswick, in the fall of '45, upon seeing our farm, it was said that Mamma was in a state of cultural shock and that she had no interest in altering her lifestyle to correspond with the shabby landscape or its people. Having had a "falling out" with her father, Mamma frequently exchanged letters with her mother back in Devon, but never mentioned Papa's criminal record or her disillusionment with our country. (She had too much pride to admit that she made a bad move.) But she often said how much there was of my grandmother, a woman I had never met, in that long-awaited mail from overseas. Around home Mamma was especially disagreeable on days like Christmas, Easter, and Thanksgiving, which brought forth special memories of the place where she grew up back in England. At such times I wondered if Papa or we children were even present in her thoughts.

Sometimes Mamma talked of leaving here, never to return, so indifferent was she to the customs. And I could see that as she grew older, she was apathetic to my father as well. It was easy to observe that her move here was more than lamentable, as back home she had attended the big private schools, had had music lessons, dance and choreography classes, roles in the school's theatrical productions, piano recitals, and was a leader in the choir at Saint Peter's Anglican church. For sure she had been a quintessentially different person back in the U.K. And then as an adventure, she left it all at the age of twenty-one to accompany a man she hardly knew to Canada. It was as if, when looking at the handsome, older man in uniform, she had invented a personality and even a Canadian landscape to please her fancy.

Here on the farm, she pushed my sisters and me to do well in school and was annoyed when we brought home a poor report card. Sometimes when she was in one of her dark moods, she asked, in secret, if we would move with her to England. I knew that she would leave Papa, but she would not leave her children, and of course we, the underlings, would never leave our father. For how do you betray someone you love, a person who has been good to you, a decent human being who has been working so hard to feed and clothe you? I knew too that if Papa was left alone here on the farm, the anguish of having lost his family would put him in an early grave. Having grown up in the wilderness, we were too much a part of *this* land to be happy or fit in anywhere else, as Mamma had not been able to adapt here. As Janet, Becky, and I walked in what we thought were the twilight years of the family circle, at times we feared Mamma would slip away in the night and we would never see her again. But she did not go.

Around home my parents never talked aloud to one another, and rarely did I hear a whisper between them. But in the nights when I peeked into their bedroom – from where I sometimes heard loud voices – I could see that Papa had his arms wrapped around her. And I thought, true love has no country. A man's strength is in the pride of his love. And when love makes a fool of him he falls into the habit of lying to himself.

I felt painfully sorry for Mamma and Papa, as I could see that both were suffering from a love that no longer existed. It was like they were tormented from an aching tooth that had already been devastatingly extracted. Or an arm that was amputated long ago, in that the person they had married was no longer there, while the memory of the good tooth or the strong arm and the feelings that accompanied them still survived. While Papa fiddled and danced to try to make it all work, grasped for fleeting coattails, Mamma cherished the past while lamenting the present and indeed the future. Her inner thoughts were always hard to fathom, because nothing could literally take the place of her recollections of home.

In the early spring of '57, long before the ice had left the river and the snow melted from our fields, my sisters, mother, and I wrote mail orders to a catalogue for fishing rods and lines and a few number two black salmon fly hooks. (In her youth Mamma had fished salmon in

Scotland.) We also sent to the village wardens for our fishing permits. Indeed, the cold season was waning, the crows had arrived, and a spirit of spring was in the air.

Mamma appeared to be excited about the coming of spring, although she was one who never showed emotion. After my father clipped her wings when she moved here – we had no money to travel abroad to see her folks – Mamma lived in a cocoon, a place in the mind that included her old home and family back in England. It was a conspiracy against the rugged outer world, her now sheltered New Brunswick life. At first she talked of the vineyards back home, of riding the South Devon (steam) Railway train that followed the river Dart to Dartmouth, the windows of the train reflecting a hundred portraits moving side by side. She spoke of having afternoon tea or perhaps fish and chips at Powderham Castle, the annual cricket matches, golf, the vine-clad brick houses with their clay chimney pots in close proximity, the red telephone booths, the yew trees that shaded the tea gardens, and the white swans on the water that triggered images of Leda and her fantasies, all so much more civilized than the mediocre scenery and habits of northeastern Canada. And then after some time she never spoke of these things anymore. She would wander off and for hours fly-fish from the shores of our farm.

While my father was well-respected after the war and was happy-go-lucky, Mamma kept the local influences locked out, even from her children. So the depth of her feelings, be they of merriment or irritation, were always incomprehensible to me. At the age of eleven, not even in reading her eyes could I detect her hostility. I now believe that she suffered long bouts of depression and spent her lifetime trying to find her true self, to enhance the life of her mind that she was so worried about, to learn how to live well and to die without regrets. But if I assumed she was in one of her dark, incensed moods, the other was likely more apparent. The simple things that she most desired on those early-rising spring mornings on the farm – our move from the main house out to the summer kitchen, black salmon angling along the shores of our great river, and the May picnic – she pretended to attach no importance to at all. But sometimes her happy moments could be detected if one carefully analyzed her actions, be they supple or fidgety. I always agreed with her, even when she contradicted me. Still, this spring, she seemed to be more into singing as she worked around our old summer kitchen in preparation for the "move out." And I said to myself: Good Heavens, Mamma is finally starting to fit in here in Canada.

Through the spring, she also kept herself busy in preparing for the picnic. This was to be held on the grassy riverbank under a huge pine tree where there was a fire pit and some wooden boat chairs placed in a circle near a salmon hole. In our family, it was a time when, at my mother's request, all the relations on my father's side – spinster aunts, bachelor uncles, nieces, nephews and cousins-by-marriage – got together at our place to celebrate the arrival of spring, Queen Victoria's birthday.

By mid May, with still some snow in the heavy woods, sunshine was penetrating the cool breeze and there was a sour smell of drying, water-soaked grass, the scent of a greening sunlight, and there was the honking of wild

geese on the river. Preparing for the Victoria Day crowd –
though they were certainly not her people – Mamma had
been baking cakes, hams, potato scallops, and had made a
variety of sandwiches. She also washed and pressed the big
red and black tablecloth, used once a year on this day, that
would be spread on the ground in the sunshine, in a place
where everyone could see up and down two bends in the
river and near where a hardwood fire would be lighted to
bake a salmon.

On the afternoon of May 24, when finally the
fire was lit, a blue smoke drifted out over the water that
sparkled like a bed of jewels. Mamma was wearing her
knee-length sundress and high-heel shoes. Papa was in his
new cotton spring trousers, while my sisters wore their
Easter dresses and I, my white shirt and denim vest.

Pockets of boisterous laughter could have been
heard for a long way on the river. Some of these people,
woodsmen, farmers, and river guides – Uncle Will was
a butcher and Uncle Jack, by his own admission, a horse
veterinarian, though without documentation – were
overweight and shabbily dressed, as they drank beer with
Papa, who appeared to be relaxed and happy to dress up
and take an afternoon off from his labour. As he sat on
a canoe seat with a beer in hand and joked with his old
friends, I could tell there was nowhere in the world that
he would rather be. There were whoops and even some
inappropriate gestures made toward the women. Old
George, our bachelor uncle from up the road – he had bad
teeth, was flushed with whisky, and with his hat falling
from his head – though not invited, brought his fiddle and
staggered around, scratching his bow in an attempt to play

some old-time ditty. When he upset the teapot, Mamma asked him to leave.

"I wish there could be a government buy-back of every Jesus fiddle in this country," she said with a glare in her eyes. "No one is going to turn this day into a hoedown."

Some children, dressed up for the occasion, were flying kites in the field in back of the riverbank. Others fished, their chrome rod-connecting ferrules glinting from the sunlight, their lines hitting the water to leave long straight splashes with a "plunk" on the hook end. Sap flies swarmed like dust mites in a sunbeam, or perhaps a cloud of locusts in a wheat field. Still, I figured that for Mamma, the sun, the laughter, and the sweet-scented breeze would have brought in its cadence the magical symbols of carousel music from the carnivals of her old home. "Oh, how I miss the aroma of English tea gardens in bloom," she had said only yesterday. "The sight of Maying brides, the ballets we used to dance to commemorate Sir Walter Scott's *Lady of the Lake*." It was one of those rare moments when she opened up and said what she was feeling.

It seemed like the more distance that grew between Mamma and the Old Country, the more extravagant the latter appeared. Her memory seemed to enhance her past, especially on days of foul weather, which were many. In what came across as a mental state, she clung to a collection of old mementos in an archivist compilation. Such are the delusions of memory. But I felt that if she would only speak more freely, more often, put her thoughts out there for all to read, we could all come to a common understanding of where she was coming from, and where she wanted to go.

Some young people played horseshoes, while a few seniors, especially the men, having carried to the river their heavy wicker baskets of food, played cards. When the last of the provisions had been brought from the trunks of cars, fresh tea had been steeped on the open fire, and the fish roasted – the fresh air having enhanced our appetites for a serving of spring salmon – we were ready to eat. People were jostling for the chairs that had been placed facing the river but away from the smoke of the fire.

"Another seven minutes," Mamma said. "There is no need for ceremony here today. Relax, have a glass of wine."

"I'll have something a little stronger meself," Uncle Charlie said.

In truth, there was not that much magic in the northeastern flowerless spring. And one had to have a good imagination to make it thus. It had been my mother's presence – she was tall and handsome with electric blue eyes – her English accent, and the fact that this was her big day that made the picnic what it was. It was like everyone had become benevolent and wanted it to be a good outing for her sake and also our family's reputation in the community, as I knew there were always rumours about Papa and Mamma not getting along. A few invitations had been sent to Mamma's reading club, as well as to her hairdresser, the Deputy Mayor of Spruce Landing, the school principal of Thornton, and the MLA for Northumberland County. And all of the in-laws who were sent invitations – most of whom were not related, but English – because of her genealogical obsessions had Mamma putting on a pensive air.

"I don't want anyone to say that I have been unfair when it came to entertaining your father's *kinfolk*," she said to me as she carved the fish with a blade from Sheffield.

We waited for the clang of the iron triangle that would signal to everyone that it was finally mealtime.

It was at this point that we noticed the downriver sky had suddenly become very dark and we heard a rumble which came from well beyond the treed horizon. Mother ignored this as if she had been waterproofed from calamity. "More wine, anyone?" she asked. It was as if for her, all the cooking and the planning, from the fish, to the wine, to the tea, with such detail had been too meticulously organized to be influenced by the weather. By God, a few raindrops are not going to keep me from celebrating this old family tradition, she might have said. And of course she wanted to make the festive moment last as this was her sovereign moment. But as the hurrying breeze suddenly made the water choppy, and black clouds drifted up the river, flashes of snakes and ladders lit up our fields in a transparent, pale-blue aurora borealis. Still, we hoped that for Mamma's sake, this little squall, with now a few raindrops sprinkling our campsite, would blow over.

We had our plates loaded up and were seated in the proper places, the Anglican priest having said the blessing, and everyone was advised to dig in. It was then that it started to rain. First there were big silver drops, one, two, three – more obvious on the water – and then it started to spill in sweeping torrents. We had to hastily gather our plates and hurry, first to get under a pine tree where we shivered from the dampness, and then to scurry back to the house where, soaked to the skin, we stood in our window-blind-darkened living room and ate our soggy meals while listening to the moan of the wind that made the awnings flap.

As Grandmamma – not a religious person except during thunderstorms – prayed, we the siblings buried our heads in feathered pillows as a hundred elephants stampeded across the sky to be pursued by cannon fire. This made the house shiver and dropped blossoms to the earth and, in the front garden, buckled the stems of the new-growth dandelions. Rain and hailstones drove from sweeping firehoses to hammer against our window glass and make the eavestroughing overflow – they were filled with petals and pollen – and uprooted the pockmarked garden's newly planted corn. Large ponds of mud glistened on the driveway as our sheep huddled under a giant tree in the pasture.

Later in the evening it was snowing. In upriver gusts of wind, the large damp flakes drifted across our open fields to stick to our buildings and trees, blot our recently hung screen doors – that led to the summer kitchen where we had moved only yesterday – so that they changed from green to white. The wind and snow sent the sheep scampering to the barn where they stood shivering under the eaves of the loafing shed. There were large chunks of slush sailing down the river and the telephone lines moaned like a harp at a winter funeral. Snow drifted off roofs and made long beards of fleece that twisted like snakes across the river intervale. It weighted down the trees and hydro lines to create a power outage. Indeed, we were back into the middle of March – it can easily happen here in May

– and we knew we had to recycle our endurance, subsist during another long wait for spring to arrive.

With a pen, paper, and a candle, I set out to work on a school essay I was writing on Thomas Hardy.

Through this, having drunk more wine, my mother played the piano, Wagner style, coming down hard on the keys, to some old air from *A Winter's Tale* that she said had been composed by Joby Talbot. It was like she was taking out her frustration on the instrument, making it dance to some complex melody that she could never master without stumbling over the most simple of measures. Her little escapes – the move to the summer kitchen, spring fishing, the May picnic, and now the music – had become re-enactments that had been filled with sentimental memories of her people and country – Hardy, Shakespeare, Wordsworth, Dorset, Stratford, Lake District influences – where as a girl she had so often gathered with family to celebrate her connections to the greater English community. As she offered now a smile, now a frown, now a grimace, it was easy to read her thoughts, her love for the symbols of bygone days. Following the colour tones in the music, these old masters and places came and went from the room. And Mamma, having tossed aside all of her formal mannerisms, and struggling now to find the keys, played on in the darkness.

Sunshine and Water

B arefoot, with sunburned arms and legs, and with our new steel trout rods in hand, my brother Dan and I walk the railway tracks. We make our way past the rust-coloured stationhouse and the brown seldom-used switch, past the Flora Weston property with its ball field and blossoming lilac trees at the front door, and on past our schoolhouse to the stone railway bridge where MacCord Brook pours through a tunnel to make a frothing waterfall. We slide down the embankment, stand on the slippery, blue boulders at the water's edge, and cast our lines into the turbulent brook that is four feet deep, covered with foam, and is flowing upstream from the back-tow. My brother has bought a number ten "bumble bee" pattern trout fly for twenty-five cents at Brown's Department Store in the village and has tied it to his four-pound test, transparent Orvis leader. I am using an angleworm.

We catch three pan-size speckled trout which I string on an alder branch. Then we follow a path along the brook that crosses a grassy elm-treed meadow to where it empties into the main river. The bubbling water of the fast-moving, smaller stream rushes out into the big wide watercourse to make glints and sparkles as it approaches the smooth water, now shaken by the wind that always announces rain, and which scatters cherry and hawthorn blossoms over the bigger flow below the brook's confluence.

Here we sit on the riverbank and share a cigarette we have stolen from our father's store. We watch the pool to see if any trout will break water where the fast-flowing brook rushes out into the slow-moving waterway. The azure June fields behind us are dappled with dandelions and daisies, and there are swallows flitting about the alder-fringed brook whose headwaters are in back of our hereditary family property; that imaginary boyhood landscape, a half-mile up the tracks and several miles back into a pine wood, where in my early childhood my father had taught me how to fish for trout. I remember, with a sense of melancholy, those magical days and places I shared with Daddy, now long dead.

A motorboat goes past, heading upstream, and its swells meet the brook's flow to make it hiss and sparkle and send tiny crystals that squirt upward and dance, before they disappear against the penetrating sunshine. It also muddies the water's edge as it laps against the sandy shore, now bleached from the sun, that has an overhang of dogwood and alder. Under these bushes, there are baby eels in the mud.

Here at the mouth of MacCord Brook is where we sometimes come to spend a pleasant summer evening while sharing the company and expertise of adults from the village who gather here to sit in the sheen of the sunset, strategize, and smoke tobacco while taking turns casting their dry-flies into the choppy brook, letting them float out into the main river and trail down a curling foam line to where we see grilse and salmon jumping and rolling upon their approach to the colder brook water. These big fish are always more active in cold water. I can remember the men telling me that. And I also remember the beautiful aroma of the blossoms.

But today there is no one here but Dan and me, and so far no fish are showing. We roll the legs of our trousers up to our thighs and wade into the ice-cold shallows. Because my brother is two years older than me, he takes the first turn and I stand beside him. Between us there is not a great physical difference, but Dan has a superiority of skill of which, at my age, I have no equivalent. He casts the bumble bee into the brook, as we have seen the adults do, and we watch as it floats out the choppy rivulet and bobs along into the curls toward the big river. When the bumble bee approaches the deeper water, a big salmon raises its head and back – for a brief moment it appears to be frozen in time – and takes the fly-hook in its mouth and goes to the bottom and holds there, bending Dan's steel rod from the wooden grip handle to the big guide at the end of the short tip.

"Wow! Ya got one on! *Dan's got a salmon on!*" I shout to the world. For a brief moment I am jealous of my brother, and I think that if I had taken the first cast, and had the bumble bee on *my* leader, this great thrill would have been mine. But this feeling is quickly overpowered by the excitement of the moment.

Dan appears to be in a trance as he stares into the gleaming water, and the fish holds to the bottom and does not move. He tells me there is a live feeling in the line and rod and that he can feel the fish breathing. Until the salmon, realizing it is hooked, starts to swim fast toward centre stream, to make the tin reel with the two-handle crank sing and then screech when the fish jumps out of the water, revealing its deep silver sides and brown back, and leaving a belly in the yellow double-tapered casting line that has turned brown under the water. The fish holds strong in the deeper currents and I say, "Dan, ya gotta reel him in – we can't let him get away! Ya gotta put some pressure on 'im. Crank, crank, *crank 'im in!*" For a split second I have an image of Dan and me carrying that big salmon up the railway to our farmhouse. For sure we would be the envy of all the children in our community

My brother does not respond. Rather he stares with popping eyes at the area where the casting line enters the water and makes a doughnut-shaped wake. And I know that he is enjoying the feel of the live fish on his hook, the breathing, like when you hold someone in your arms. Finally, the fish swings and comes fast toward the shore and Dan is scrambling to pick up the slack line. He cranks as fast as his little hands can turn the reel handles, and we get a brief look at the fish, coppered slightly by the water, a good twenty pounds, silver-sided and wide across the back, with a deep rubber tail. But then, seeing us, the fish turns quickly and heads back out into the big river. "Dan," I say, "we can't let 'im go back out there. We can't land a big fish like that in the middle of the river." For a quick moment I want to jump into the water and swim after it, as it had been in so close to shore for a while, which gave me the impression that it would soon be ours to carry up those sun-heated, rust-smelling railroad tracks.

This time the salmon takes a longer run, as though it is being jet propelled, and Dan tries to put some pressure on the backing to slow it down. But I can see that he is running out of line, and fast. When the spool is bare, the line tightens and Dan has to hold onto the rod so as not to lose it in the river. And with the short rod bent double, the line as taut as a fiddle string, my brother is cutting a precise image, like those old Norman Rockwell printings we used to see on farm calendars, depicting a barefoot boy with his shirttail out, bracing against the pressure of an oversized fish on the end of a line, or perhaps by a dog that is tugging at the seat of his pants.

When the backing goes slack, we know the fish has gone free. There is an empty feeling shared, as Dan reels in the line to see that the bumble bee is missing, the leader having broken at the knot. "It's all your fault," he says with anger in his words. He pushes me out of the way. "You and your big mouth, always telling me what to do!"

"But you were going to let it ..."

For a brief moment I am ashamed of how I acted and want to take back my words. And because I am crying, my brother hugs me. Dejected, we head up the tracks, each of us reliving the experience, one sleeper step at a time. It had been a day that, for a short time, held so much promise, so much excitement. It would live inside us for a long time. It was an experience that brought us back to this same spot, real or imagined, to go through the same routine many times afterwards.

While I have hooked and landed a thousand salmon since, most of which I cannot remember, seventy-odd years later, I can recall every detail of that little fishing experience with my brother. In my mind's eye, under similar conditions, every detail is present, like the cherry trees and bird songs of childhood, the family get-togethers of former times, perhaps brought to mind by a certain, though fleeting, image. Sometimes it comes out of a blossom scent from the field, at other times a wind that makes the water in front of my cabin sparkle – a rehashing of recollections that come out of a childhood experience that was bigger than life. I can still see it. I can taste it. I can smell it. In reminiscence, I recapture every move the big fish made; every reposition my brother reacted to; the great excitement that befell two children on that June afternoon of '52. It is all bathed in sunlight and water.

Sometimes I wonder if it all might have been a dream.

Spring Waters

When the long-awaited migrating birds have returned, the last decaying chunks of river ice have melted from along the shores, pine and spruce logs are being rolled into the river for driving, and the poplar trees are sprouting a mouse's ear of new leaf, my mother asks if I will go and catch a salmon, as we have no fish for the Good Friday supper. It is that time in the spring when the heat from the kitchen wood range is still appreciated and my mother is into housecleaning. Outside, the scent of cat urine is strong in the woodshed, and the barn's smell of cow manure, potent now in the dampness, can be detected from our front veranda where the fibreglass fishing rods hang on moose antlers.

On this dark, rainy day in early May, I bundle up and, grabbing my fishing rod, stomp down the flat to the old wire bridge. There are still patches of snow in the swamp in back of the brown field with its map-shaped patches of ash from the grass fires. Because of the wetness, there is a sour smell in the meadow along the pathway; it mixes with the ash to bring a dump-fire odour. I labour up the weather-beaten plank steps and, feeling the dampness of the river, hearing the freshet sounds, I make my way across the shaky spans, staggering against the flapping cables, looking down at the big rain-dappled, smooth-flowing river, so near the boards, and in a state of dizziness, look across to see Harold Gray on the far side. He is casting his self-made buck-tail streamer out into the curls of Charlie's eddy.

My mother has told me many times to not look down when crossing the wire bridge, especially when the water is this high. Rather I should hang onto the cables, stare at the opposite hillside to keep the bridge from moving upstream at the speed of the water that spills around the centre abutment to make a wake and a foam-line that trails downriver for a long way.

Sometimes when the water is low and the black salmon are in the middle of the river, I fish from the bridge, walking back and forth with the transparent leader, casting line, and some of the thread-like backing that swings far below me, although it is illegal to do this. From this vantage point, I can see a fish chasing after my fly-hook for a long way off.

Once in late spring, Harold and I set a gaspereau net under the bridge where Harold sat on a bench and smoked tobacco. Because he was night blind, he could not see two inches down into the dark water. From up on the bridge I could detect the fish coming up the river in schools. They made a little wake as they travelled over the shallows, and I threw rocks into the river to scatter them out into the net. With the boat, Harold took them out of the two-inch fine-twine mesh and put them into a five-gallon galvanized drum to be shared by both families. We got our winter's supply of gaspereau that way.

Now I can see that Harold has built a small fire on the ground, behind some short, scrubby pine trees. The blue smoke filters through the tree branches and drifts out over the water. And there is the splash of his heavy streamer as it hits the water – like a .22 bullet – well out at the edge of the fast-moving river. When I get to the eddy, he does not speak; rather he keeps casting and retrieving his fly-hook, the coils of the casting line wound round his left hand. And I think, it is not necessary for me to break his spell, no need for words just now.

Over the driftwood fire hangs a black pail of bubbling brown tea and in the dead grass there is a tattered raincoat and a pack of Players tobacco and papers. (Harold is wearing his mackinaw coat and stocking-leg cap.) It is always a few degrees colder here at the river, I think, as I warm my hands and roll myself a smoke, lighting it with a brand from the flame. The cigarette makes me cough as I am too young to be a full-time smoker and only have one when I fish with Harold. Sometimes he scolds me for using his tobacco without asking, and at other times he is offended if I ask him for a smoke. He is never the same character two days in a row. It depends on what frame of mind he brings to the river, and if he is here for healing, or just to catch a fish.

"Day," I say.

"Day."

"See any?"

He holds up four fingers, so I know he has caught four salmon and released them. He is not here for the fish, rather just to be at the river, even on this raw day, especially on this raw spring day. He knows too that at this time of day, I have come here to take home a fish for the supper table, and because he has already caught many, he moves up the shore to give me the hot spot at the mouth of Charlie's Brook.

This is where the big spring salmon hang out, right in close to the dogwood, alder, and willow bushes that grow out into this water. And using a weighted-down hook that Harold has tied – he has wrapped a thin strip of sheet lead along inside the body of the hook – I cast as far as I can, out into the moving stream, and stroke the streamer toward me in spurts, letting it go low, sometimes catching my hook on the bushes, freeing it by stripping in the line and poking at the hook with the tip of my rod, before casting again. Until from a long deep-swinging cast, I feel a pull from the depths and see a swirl. I set the hook by holding the line and jerking the rod into a semi-circle. I holler above the water sounds, "There's one." And Harold reels in his line to give me a hand in landing the fish.

I move back on the shore and hold my rod high so that Harold can work under the line and get down to the water's edge and grab the brown fish from the brown water as soon as it tires and comes near the surface so that only its white mouth with the yellow streamer can be seen. And for a time we can see only the streamer. The salmon holds deep and circles the eddy many times before nosing up to the shore grass, its narrow back out of water. Finally, Harold is able to grab the fish by its tail and half swing, half toss it up into the grass so that I can wrestle it down and take the hook out of its gaping, wood-like jaws. The fish is a good eight-pounder that would have weighed twelve pounds the summer before when it first came up the river to spawn. These fish are always losing weight in the fresh water.

"Headin' back over?"

"Headin' back over."

Having finished my smoke, I pick up my fish by the gills and strike out across the wire bridge and up the flat to home. Few words have been spoken by either of us, but they were good communication and a great deal could be taken as understood. It is a kind of game we play, boys against fish; river sounds against idle chatter. And I think of the words of Norman MacLean: "A river has many things to say and it's hard to know what it says to each of us."

At home, the salmon is cleaned and cut into steaks. My mother, having rolled them in flour, puts them into the big doughnut-frying pan, a maple stick in the stove. The steaks sizzle and the skin turns crisp to make a smoke in the kitchen. And for a brief moment she opens the door to let the smoke escape. The steaks are placed on a platter to be put on the big oil-cloth-covered table and served with fresh fiddleheads, a sprinkle of vinegar, a squeeze of lemon, and half-peeled potatoes. A salmon is a great treat at this time of the year, even a black one. Later in the evening, the leftovers are enjoyed with the wide, heavy slices of homemade bread and molasses, to be mopped up and savoured with a cup of black bulk tea from the kettle that is always singing on our kitchen range.

And in this taste there are symbols of the river. She is a grand old mother, a provider, a healer, a place of recreation, of commerce, of security, of home and family, and of good times.

And I think that it is good to live on the banks of a great river.

The Love Tree

Under that old pine tree the ground was an orange cushion of needles with decaying buds that looked like Churchillian cigars. It was a place to lie and look up at the extended gray limbs, elephant trunks that reached so far toward heaven. The whispering needles appeared silver against the afternoon sunlight and there was sighing among the top branches, a kind of murmur, even when there was no wind. It made my mind soar free into the cloudless upper air. It was a location where I loved to go to relax and meditate, a place that loved me back, especially in the sultry winds of late summer and early autumn. The high branches cast green shadows on the spills, like when the sun shines through a leafy window curtain to make broken patterns on the parlour floor.

Up there on that breezy hilltop, with its patchwork of small clearings from former times – dooryard, barnyard, and garden – and with the spreading woods around me, I could see for a distance of two bends in the big river that sparkled far below, the fresh air being good for my asthma. So I went there often, sometimes alone, but frequently with my grade eight friend. Though well-born, beautiful, intelligent, and with a virgin ear in all its innocence, Jill Anderson was a dear companion in that we thought alike and had a passion for lonely places where everything was natural. And I clung to her like ivy clings to a brick chimney. We were always looking to escape the school crowd and to be alone, together with nature. (Many great relationships have grown out of lesser experiences.) Sometimes we went there during April, when we shared the most extremities of passion.

The property was owned by a rich government official who lived in the capital city. It had been said that it was an acreage that the game of chance had brought his way, a place he never visited for any reason other than to look at the woods and wonder what the trees' worth would be at the sawmill.

Not far from this pine tree was a decaying cement foundation, the house having burned many decades before our time. In front of what had once been a lilac arbour stood a rusted wrought-iron bench, the kind found in city gardens. I remember sitting with Jill on that bench and sharing a box lunch that my mother had prepared for us, sweet moments to be relived a thousand times since. Nearby, among some tall spruce stood two apple trees, one of which in autumn was loaded down with purple Queen's Choice crabs and the other with little winter, marble-size apples that never ripened, even in the late fall. According to my mother the latter was good only for preserving. And I can remember their tangy flavour under our homemade ice cream on a Thanksgiving Sunday. But we went there, Jill and I, to share the spirit and freedom of the setting –

like special people, pine trees have a spirit all of their own – to meditate, and to fill our shirts with the bigger apples to take home to our mothers. These would be put into our school lunches to be tasted at recess time and for a brief moment be carried away to that special river place.

To get to this spot we took my father's board boat, poling from home a half-mile against the flow in the heavy currents and going ashore on the rocky beach near a quicksand which we were careful to step around. We followed an old overgrown wagon road that was cut slash-wise to scar the hillside, having taken with us the long canoe pole that would be used for knocking the apples down without bruising them.

One time we went there when the apple blossoms could be scented from the river and I made a bouquet for Jill. And in my childish, uncultured ways – my mother was a housemaid and my father a country singer who sang at the Legion dances in town and each of whom had sentimental longings – I was torn between my many reasons for being there, like a child who jumps from toy to toy on Christmas morning. I wanted to pray and meditate; I loved the scent of the kind-smelling blossoms, the tangy flavour of the apples, the constant whispering of the great pine tree.

But most of all I enjoyed Jill's well-bred countenance, because she brought with her a spirit that was carefree and heartwarming and with a graceful ease and loveliness so natural to her when no one was around but me. I admired all the aspects of her beauty, one by one: her dark penetrating eyes – I had never seen more attractive eyes – her curly black hair, her cute giggle. They fell upon me like so many apples from different branches and at various times. She had a nobility of soul, provincial good sense, and a kindness for everyone. She was also quick-tempered, and would "flare up" like a half-smothered fire. When this happened she spoke in a higher octave than usual, concert pitch. This authentic spirit would remain at this river place long after she had moved on from our little one-room school to explore bigger and better places abroad and which eventually led her to a professorship at Holy Cross. One day she just went away and she never came back. Her persona changed from a voice to an echo, and then an echo of an echo, a resonance that lived on in the whisper of pine needles so that for brief moments I could see the wind in her hair, the sparkle in her eyes.

Early on, I realized that it had been Jill Anderson's influence that made the river place what it was: her wholesome country soul, the quality of her innocent mind, her sensitive response to the whispering of pine needles. "It's like Mozart's music," she had said. As if yielding to such emotion was good, not only for artists, but sentimentalists too. When she mentioned Milton's Paradise, there was no question of her superiority. Jill and I lay on the soft needles, side by side in a platonic delight, so close we were touching. On this, the sunniest day in the summer, lifted so far above the earth by the melodious pine breezes, I dreamed of us someday getting married under this tree. For to possess the one we love is as great a joy as the love itself. I thought of how attractive she would look in a wedding dress, and I said to myself, "Soon I must tell her that I love her."

The pitch on the needles made them stick to our shirts and shorts that had to be brushed clean when we stood up. And I found there was an indescribable pleasure in doing this for her. Sometimes I would put an arm around her and kiss her beautiful cheeks, which made her blush. At other times I kissed her smooth, sunburned arms, as if to separate the material from the ethereal, to see how the mix would be, and if they would come together with a gentle touch. Jill always wore cut-off jeans, even though the disagreeable old priest up at the mission scolded her for wearing shorts into church where we sometimes went together – Jill played the organ – and where the women sat in the pews and the men stood at the back. This was where Father Goodin, the best-read man on the river, had been tutoring Jill in theology and music. (He sidled around the pews, like a character in an old Poe story, the slap-slip-slip of his tread informing us that under his cassock he was wearing slippers.)

Now from our state of repose under the pine tree, we could hear the shallow peal from that bell tower that could be seen in the distance, white against the cool green woods and quiet fields of the river valley. And for a moment it distorted our young dreams, as the crowing of the cock had aroused Saint Peter. It was time for us to go home.

Before we left the shade of the pine tree to return to the boat, we filled our shirts with apples, having tied the shirttails into knots, exposing our bellies, to make a kind of hammock. And we made our way back to the river, laden with the apple-size pine-tree-moments to be relived with each bite.

For years, when I went to that river place alone, the breeze, the whisper of needles, the murmur of branches brought that unique Jill Anderson atmosphere back to me, the Mozart music, the lost Paradise. Yes, for these reasons the tree had drawn me there. Plus, as we grow older, our love for repose increases and the glory lies not so much in being loved, but in loving. I am an expert when it comes to dealing with rejection, lost love.

While Jill has long since gone from my life, as an aged man I see her here as of old: a young woman who never lost sight of who she really was, or where she was heading. (Sometimes I wished I could have heard something bad about her so that I could diminish my perception of her purity, but these things never came and she remained perfect in every way, impossible to lose faith in. And I felt that in her life of absence she was being loyal to me so I hung onto her memory as a place to go.) I can still scent the fragrance of her summer dress, the apple blossom in her hair; see the autumn shirt filled with apples, hear her tender voice in the whispering branches. Save for a distorted phone call here and there, her journey into maturity, the university years, remains untold. Why look back, she might have said. These reflections became a state of self-preservation after I heard that, at the age of seventy, she had died of cancer in a Boston hospital.

The pine tree spirit is still carried inside me, even when I am somewhere else and alone, especially when I was somewhere else alone. Through my flowerless adult life, working the factories, I savoured that solitude: the memorable atmosphere, the music, and my untold love for Jill Anderson with her wonderful honesty, which had become synonymous with the scent of blossom, the taste of an apple, the whisper of a tree. I dreamed about our great times beneath the wonderful pine that had been such a resolute stalwart and a landmark in our community for all the generations. Indeed it stood tall and strong, a symbol of my love for Jill.

Until, more recently, I went there one autumn day to find that someone had cut down the great tree, sawed it into logs, and, I assumed, trucked it away to the sawmill, closing the book on the symbol of my after-years with Jill Anderson. Yes, it had been cut down like an old lover that is suffering with young, wistful longings. And I said to myself, "Just like vandals." I counted the rings in the table-size stump, over two hundred and fifty, the outer ones being closer together because of the slowing down of growth through the aging process. I wondered if the tree's value at the mill would be worth as much to the owner as it had been (left standing) for people like Jill Anderson and me. These things I would never know as trees mean different things to different people, either harvested or standing alive. There are few such trees left on the landscape, few reflective symbols, real or imagined. But for me, this one will live on, the whispering spirit of a true love from long ago.

River Places

There was a drowsiness in the classroom, the heat of a spring afternoon penetrating the tall, twentieth-century windows. It filled the school with a sense of lethargy. At the back of the room, out of earshot from the teacher, there was whispering, the sharing of notes, and the copying of essays. But I was not really into studies and only habit and a little discipline kept me at my desk. (Of course, to my teacher I was still the same pupil as always.) I glanced out the window at the choppy water, so full of life, the trees in bud along the bank of the big river so near on that happy side of the school. In my mind I was already on my way to the Cavanaugh eddy, an escape that was ever-present in my daydreams, especially in the months of April and May. That old river place, so full of wonder, was like a guardian angel to me: it nourished my soul, inspired my imagination, and lifted me out of the stuffy, chalk-scented environment – that old three-windowed, clapboard schoolhouse.

Barefoot and with a peeled juniper fishing pole, black fish-twine wound around and around the butt end, a can of angleworms, and with an old country song on my mind, I made my way up the river intervale, skirting around the recently sown oat fields – with the ghost of my father in farm boots, loose trousers, and flannel shirt, walking behind the horse-drawn harrow – hopped over the line-fence to the dry and sour-smelling Cavanaugh field that was sprouting grass in a place where my brother and I sometimes played horseshoes. I hurried past the old black hay-barn and on out toward the riverbank with its big white-pine tree – it had twisted and kinked roots, bare on the river side – with its elbows, knees, and reaching arms that were scarred by the ice flows. This, the mother of all trees, centuries old, leaned over the water to shade the mother of all eddies that was foam-covered as it curled and twisted so that within its perimeters, the river was flowing in circles. Spooked by my approach I could hear the "plop" of frogs and turtles as they jumped into the water.

Feeling the warmth of the sun and river winds, hearing the warble of a robin, the tune of an April song sparrow that was singing to me and me alone, I sat on the shore in the warm sand and baited my hook before casting thirty feet of line into the outer reaches of the eddy to let it sink and await the tug of a speckled trout or even a grilse that would justify my reason for being here. The morning was agreeable and pleasant, and there was the lowing of distant cattle as I sat and watched the big river flow past with a whisper. It seemed to say, this is where you belong young fellow, let us enjoy the day together. The spirit of that river place always brought with it a distinct pleasure and I was protective in disallowing any omens to the contrary.

Upriver about fifty yards, and forty feet out into the water, stood the Cavanaugh Rock, a minivan-size landmark, high above the water, where a woman of the community used to sometimes sit with a crowbar and watch for the fish wardens to come down the river while below her, around the bend, the men drifted with gill nets to get their winter's supply of salmon for salting. When the woman saw the wardens approaching by canoe, she pounded the rock with the steel bar, making a church-bell-like peal that could be heard for miles along the water and which gave the men plenty of time to gather their nets and fish and get off the river. This great rock was also a landmark for the men who, in low water, sometimes had their horses wade across the river while tugging their loaded truck-wagons, following a bar that extended slash-wise, from shore to shore, as they made their way to the old Mill Road that took them to Canes River, a tributary where they were lumbering. The table-size rock was also a place to lie and get a suntan after swimming in the eddy when the water was lukewarm in summer. Indeed, this river place was a big part of my dreams, my culture, and my livelihood.

This is where, as a boy, one evening in April my father was sitting on the end of a moored boat, casting a line into the water and catching a few trout for the breakfast table when suddenly a bull moose, being chased by dogs, came galloping over the riverbank. It struck the boat and splintered it into a thousand pieces, knocking Papa into the eddy. Because he could not swim, he had to grab what was left of the boards and paddle himself to shore. He was in a state of shock, but unharmed as he watched the big animal swim the river and disappear into the trees on the far side.

This is where in the dog days of August, as children, my cousins and I baited our hooks with silver chub and cast our lines out into the deep hole to catch eels which, with our young arms, were almost impossible to lift out of the water. These fish held to the bottom like sunken logs. On one occasion, a cousin from up the road caught an eel and was able to drag it to the shore. Because she was afraid of the snake-like fish, she ran screaming from the river with the eel trailing after her. In her panic she did not realize that the fish was still on the hook and she was dragging it, and that it was *not* chasing her but being pulled by her. Indeed, with our young imaginations, strange things happened at this river place.

And it must be said that this was also a place to escape to for a bit of healing when things were not going well around home. And I cannot begin to tell you how often I came here for that reason alone. Sometimes the most subtle impressions are the ones that are printed most clearly in memory.

On this morning in May, feeling the wind tugging my clothes, the rain sprinkling my face, I came here to the eddy. Trout and salmon were flipping on the surface near the outer perimeters. I fished with bait and caught six speckled trout that I took home to my mother, who would fry them up for the evening meal. At that time Johnny Gray was living at our house, having had a disagreement with his mother, who lived across the river on a hill at the end of the bridge. (My mother was always quick to take in wayward people who needed a home and a little affection. She had the biggest heart of any woman I ever knew.) At our house, Johnny – he said that he always felt at home with our family – sat in the living room, smoked tobacco, and listened to the radio soap operas. And his garments smelled of grime and tobacco smoke. He was ten years older than me and had lost a leg and an arm in a motorcycle accident in April of '51. When he saw the trout I had caught, he asked if I would take him to the eddy, build a lean-to from poles, start a fire, and sit out of the rain to fish and smoke his tobacco through the afternoon. Of course I jumped at the offer.

After lunch, we dressed and made our way to the eddy, with Johnny swinging forward on his long crutch as he walked. He complained about the aches and pains that were coming from his missing leg and arm, a condition that would have been a physiological reaction from wounds suffered in the accident before the limbs had been amputated. Carrying an axe and a small roll of tarpaper, I was happy to be with Johnny, who would not let me go fishing with him if my older brother Jimmy was around. I knew this was the only chance I had to fish with someone his age, uncontested, as neither one had a choice in the matter because it was the spring of '52 and Jimmy was working down at the sawmill. And if Johnny wanted to get out of the house on a rainy day in May, he would have to come with me. With the lean-to made of poles and covered with tarpaper, we built a fire of pitch-wood limbs from the pine tree, baited our hooks, and sat on a log with our lines in the water. We sat through the gray and drizzling afternoon and on toward evening, but never got a nibble. It was cold and our shelter leaked. After some time, we realized that the water was rising because of the rain. My father told me many times that fish would not take a baited hook in water that was coming up. This was something that was proven to Johnny and me that afternoon.

Finally, Johnny asked me to put a fly-hook on his leader and after a few casts hooked a grilse which he landed and immediately sold, for one dollar, to a man passing by in a motorboat. "This is enough money to buy me two packs of cigarettes," he said. And I thought that it was selfish of him to sell the fish, as we could have used it at home for a special meal, as he was eating at our house for free.

It was here under the lean-to, with the rain coming down, that the fishing lines were soon forgotten when Johnny told me about his former love – she was the only woman to really capture his heart – who lived a mile down the highway. She had moved on from his troubled life not long after the accident and he was living in a state of shock. "No woman wants half a man," he said with a self-deprecatory, forced smile that revealed a missing front tooth. And the natural setting, so pure, added to the sincerity of our conversation. I wondered if Johnny had come here for healing himself. (For sure it was a situation that took careful handling. Also, I did not want to tarnish the spirit of the place with a discussion on a sad predicament like a broken heart.) "I have sowed my share of wild oats," he told me. "But it was only through that woman that I could find true happiness, a meaningful life. She meant the whole world to me." He stared into the bosom of the river where fingerlings darted about at the edge of the shore grass.

I could remember Johnny, before the accident, when he was dating this young woman, and how happy-go-lucky he had been when they came to my father's store to sit and talk with his river chums. And I thought that maybe his girlfriend's loss, along with the disagreements he had had with his parents, were the reasons he was mean to me when my brother was around, and that he needed only one friend – someone he could really confide in, heart to heart – and that was Jimmy. So I knew what he had been like and what he would be like again when Jim came home. And deep down inside, I understood his lover's estrangement.

"But could there not be some happiness found in loving someone who does not love you back?" I ventured.

"No! I could never love a woman who betrayed me. No, no – I would do my best to make her unhappy."

How cynical, I thought.

"I got to find a way to be alive again, that's all, if there is such a thing." He looked at me with those moistened brown eyes that appeared to be so filled with pain. And for years afterwards when I went to that river place, I could see those troubled eyes staring at me as if from out of the water.

Disappointed at the end of the afternoon we left the dampness of the river, the sad conversation, and made our way back home with Johnny limping, more obviously now, and complaining about his good leg and good arm also aching. At home in our warm kitchen, my mother prepared the trout that I caught in the morning. With a candle burning, she fried them to a crisp, the way I used to like them, occasionally opening the kitchen door to let the smoke drift out of the room. But the grilse that Johnny had caught and sold and the story of a lost love – both had somewhat tarnished the atmosphere of the eddy – were never mentioned. The trout were served in the big dining room to a full table, with Johnny among us, with potatoes, pancakes, and eggs. Johnny Gray was a big part of our family when I was a kid.

Later that summer Johnny moved back to his mother's house. And I can remember Jimmy going with him to carry his straw suitcase as they made their way across the bridge and up the long hill to where his mother, standing on the doorstep, embraced him. Later that summer Johnny sold tickets on his Indian 134 Series motorcycle and a raffle was held at my father's store, with the winning ticket going to a man from upriver. This man immediately gave the bike back to Johnny. Later it was sold outright to a young woman in Stanton and the money given to Johnny's folks, who set out to purchase an artificial leg for him. I can remember seeing Johnny's father poling their flat board-boat up the river to Papa's store, with Johnny sitting in the front, paddling, paddling with one arm, hard against the flow. And their voices were just barking sounds against the rushing of the water. But things appeared to have gone back to normal. Anger is caused by fear, I thought.

But in less than a year, we got the news that Johnny Gray had developed cancer of the lungs and he was dead in a matter of months. I was glad that I had not pined over a lost love, could not afford tobacco, and had not travelled with him more. I urged my brother to give up the cigarettes and get a chest x-ray.

Of course these things happened over sixty-five years ago, although they are as fresh in my mind now as they were in the days following the spring of '52. Years later, I would realize Johnny's pain when I experienced a similar heartache. As a drummer, I had gone to Quebec to look for work in a nightclub. I had a plan to send for my lover, Helen, when I found work. Having been away for four weeks, on a Saturday night, travelling on a bus out of Sherbrook, I came home to surprise her. Upon my arrival in town, finding that she was not at home, I went down the street to a bar where we used to hang out. Looking in a window, I saw Helen being bounced about on the knees of a former cop, a man who had a reputation as a womanizer. I was too shocked to go inside; rather I went back to the bus stop where I purchased a ticket back to Quebec. She would never know why I never returned. But losing the love of that young woman brought me a state of mind that I carried inside for the rest of my life. Like Johnny Gray's predicament, it was a despair that would never go away.

Now, as a senior citizen – for old age comes upon us overnight – I grasp backwards for the recollections of an innocent boyhood. (For an elderly bachelor is the loneliest and most pathetic of men. He despises the well-born and the shallow, while defending the sense of his own inner pride.) As of old, on the weekends, I return from the city to this river place for healing. Here the sleeping waters make but a whisper, the noble winds still young and crisp. I try to grasp some of the heart feelings from before I tasted real love, so cruel. Saturday nights in the country hold many recollections for me. And I now believe that the emotions we shared in our young lives were the most dramatic of them all, as these were the feelings from which our lives were invented.

As I sit alone at the Cavanaugh eddy with a line in the water – which justifies my being here – those youthful experiences, their distinct impressions, come back to me in pockets. It is a different river now with fewer fish and fewer people – most of my friends are now sleeping on the grassy hillside by the church. We have killed so much in our search to fulfill young dreams that were always beyond reach, no matter how successful we had become, and of course to follow the trends. And the fields that Papa had spent his lifetime tilling have grown into a big wood. The rambling old farmhouse and barns have been torn down, as has our little one-room school, the train station, post office, and my father's general store. The songbirds have also disappeared. Indeed, it has become a place for an old person to retreat from the viruses of modern times: old dreams and old events to be recycled, at the close of day, yes, in the waning autumn years of one's fragile life.

For this night, I stay at my father's log cabin, a dream camp he built in '49 when I was six years old and in grade one. I can remember him with a broad axe, hewing out the beams and the side logs, dovetailing the corners to make them strong. The camp now appears smaller and is a bit sunken, but its wall hangings and stone fireplace offer me a sense of comfort I cannot find in town. The scent of burning logs takes me back to my early boyhood when on November mornings Papa and I built fires in the woods to warm ourselves and to make tea while hunting deer. The log walls embrace me and I meditate as to where in the woods each has grown, my father's labour in cutting them down.

In an old gilded, ornate frame, there is a ghost of yesterday: Mamma in a low-cut dress with a necklace of pearl beads at her throat, according to that year's fashion, and her blond hair and pink hands clasping a vase of lilacs, in bloom – a portrait done by Papa when they were young, on a gray afternoon in June when the light was the same hue all day. It was a painting of which my dear mother was so proud. The artwork signed "William" was deemed a masterpiece in our little family circle. Papa was a sentimentalist; I can see that in Mamma's features. And I can remember him saying, "Your mother was tired that day." These were profound impressions to which deep thought gave real meaning.

It had been painted in the old-fashioned manner of working people, his finest period, so provincial, before he took art lessons in town, among people who were in class because they were simply looking for an audience, or perhaps money. And since this work was valued by family as Papa's most heartfelt likeness of Mamma, it remained here at the old cabin, a small attempt to display Father's humble vision of grandeur which could not be taught in the village art class. And while I am not a connoisseur of fine art, I can see in it my mother, in one of her melancholy moments, as I had so often observed her in real life. It brought back the voice of old school and church, her refined elegance. "A lovely face," I said aloud. "Mamma never ate; rather she always dined."

Of course the painting was one-dimensional and failed to capture her love for the family, her love for life, which she was so filled with. It was a part of history I had almost forgotten and which was brought back to mind, no doubt, because of the painting. Of course the artwork would be worthless to anyone outside the immediate family, all of whom have long since passed on. There had been lesser hangings: the old apple tree in bloom, the pasture gate choked by clematis, our well-house in the trees, all of which among family had become bones of contention, but all agreed that this portrait of Mamma should remain here at dream camp.

Now I grasp for other images of Mamma, the quality of her soul that might appear in a symbol, the distinct impression of a taste, a smell, a touch that could possibly bring her back for a brief moment. But these are things that one cannot make happen; rather they fall upon us when the moment and the symbol unite and for a brief moment she appears. When I am in a melancholy state of mind, my mother can emerge in something as subtle as the tinkle of a wind chime, the chirp of a blackbird in the camp trees, an old song on the car radio, or the murmur of a church organ. But it is all so long ago she lived, forcing the issue now is like trying to find the ticking of a clock that is hiding, perhaps under a cushion, in a big room full of cushions and ticking clocks. And I think that one cannot make these vignettes appear; they have to come to us on their own, and within a split-second's grasp of an image, like the writing of fiction.

In an old black-and-white photograph beside a bronze clock on the mantle stands our family: Mamma, Papa, Grandmother, Grandfather, and us two children, dressed for church, waiting for a taxi while standing on the lawn, under our big elm tree. Johnny Gray is in a white shirt and white pants, with one trouser leg and one arm cut off, folded over and held in place with big safety pins, as he leans on crutches to stand next to my brother Jimmy – all equal members of our family. And there is Grandfather, leaning on his cane, having suffered horse-riding fractures in his youth, the cold country houses, the ruptures and the rheumatism that come from a life of hard work.

From that old day, there are so many places and times that are conducive to memory, so many heartstrings to grasp for. They are like symbols of the river that might come from out of the taste of a fishcake, or perhaps a garden scene that vibrates from the flavour of freshly cut lettuce. And suddenly we are all together again in that old place and time. The same may be said about the fragrance of certain perfumes or spices that might bring someone from out of the past. This might be found on a stranger in a shopping mall, on the city transit, or in an open market, and suddenly I can see Mamma getting dressed in her new outfit, with her big spectacles, a necklace, and with her felt hat tilted down in the front, before going to sing in the choir of our little country church now long gone. Perhaps she is wearing a straw hat, while on her knees weeding her flower garden, or a red bandana while making pickles in the kitchen. (These simple impressions cannot be planned or reinvented and would be featureless to anyone else.) Back then, each part of her dress code appeared to be for a particular setting – a dance, a wedding, a funeral, a stint in the fields, a day in the kitchen – and carried the spirit of her commitment to each, that particular aspect of her essence that was so favourable to all who knew her. It is like nature had taken a lesson from art.

My mother is still a constant study, as is Johnny Gray. They are brought to me now in a thousand overlapping recollections, triggered perhaps by the aforementioned subtleties, golden pumpkins that glisten on a plane of lesser yields. And hearing the pleasure of the old clock chiming again on the hour, the whistle of a distant train in the starlit wood, a conveyance by which Mamma had travelled to and from the city on so many occasions, I take a pill, get into the familiar old bed, and enjoy a sleep that is sent from Heaven.

Youth Home

Behind the County Home the big river flowed in slow motion. On April nights the dimpled water moved smoothly and the ferry to Bradford laboured across to where cattle grazed and their little bells tinkled in the darkness. Toads sang, and in the breeze, music drifted along the shore from the Legion Hall down on King Street. Paula and I smoked tobacco and fished chubs in the eddy, the cigarettes' glow lighting up our young, twilight faces. The old river, which stayed pink long after sunset, brought us a sense of freedom. In summer, on nights of full moon, we lay on the sand and listened to the waves that were breaking and receding. We always swam after dark because we had no bathing suits. And we always felt better after being in the water. It seemed to wash away the torments of Hayward, the headmaster who kept us awake at night, and it helped us get rid of the hatred that grew out of the rules that were forced upon us by the Children's Foundation Committee. When things built up inside us, we went to the river, where in a haze of tobacco smoke and mist we talked things out before baptizing ourselves.

Hayward was right about one thing: a good dousing appeared to wash away *his* sins. We did this until the fall came and the chilly rains fell in a gray upriver slant and the wind bent the trees and made black waves pound the wharf down on Canterbury Street where the fishing boats were tied.

At the beginning of winter, before the river froze all the way across, in the twilight after school, we skated on board-ice along the edges of the black alder shores. (There had been skates left at the house by orphans who lived there before us.) We built bonfires on the frozen beach to warm our hands and feet, the sun having gone behind the trees to leave a copper horizon on the far side. At this time of year, the wharf rats came from the river to our slop hole. I fired rocks at them with my sling shot. When snow came, to make a crust along the shore, rats found their way into the house and crawled between the plastered walls. Through the night, I could hear them running in the attic. Paula was afraid of rats and once, when she saw one in her room, peed in her pajamas. Screeching, she ran down the hall to wake up Maria, the housemaid. It brought us all out of our beds to bump into one another in the hallway. It might have been a fire drill. After that I was assigned the duty of rat patrol. I set the wooden Victor traps in the cellar and caught a few.

Rat holes made the big house drafty. On winter nights as the place creaked in the wind we burned pine slabs in the parlour Franklin. But because Hayward was afraid of chimney fires, he let the stoves burn low in the early evening. Windows frosted over, urine in chamber pots turned to lemon jelly, and the water in buckets on the kitchen washstand became preserver's wax. The hand-pump froze solid, its long arm reaching upright like the Statue of Liberty. Sometimes in the night when everyone was sleeping, I sneaked down the stairs and put a stick in the parlour stove, the fragrance of which took me back to my boyhood in Collin's Bay. The fire blinked orange upon the old pump organ and the gilt picture frames of make-believe family.

In the cellar, where I went to check my traps after school, I found a flask of whisky hidden in the woodpile. Without a second thought I poured it out, peed in the bottle, and put it back where I got it. I would have given anything to see Hayward drink my piss. He never mentioned the incident. I figured he did not want anyone to know he kept booze in the so-called Christian Youth Home. But at the supper table he glared at me and I could see the anger in his eyes. Once I overheard him say to Maria about Paula and me, "Those two brats belong in a reform school."

I told this to the nuns from St. Andrew's Convent when they came to pray with my surrogate sister and me. Sister Connors said we should not listen to him when he degraded us; rather we should learn the catechism, receive our First Communion, and get confirmed because we were by then twelve years old. The priest from St. Paul's, who came on a bicycle at Christmas, did not preach. Instead he gave us fudge he had made at the rectory. While he was at the house, Hayward put on a kind face and talked like he was a gentleman.

Paula said, "It's not about what someone shows in public, it's what they do to us in private that matters."

When the priest was gone, Hayward passed me a shovel. "Here, goofball, clean the snow from the driveway," he said. "That should keep you out of mischief for a while."

I wanted to spend more time outside anyway.

On the downriver side of the house, towards Albert Street, there was a barn with three cows, two of which I fed, watered, and milked daily. This, with my school lessons, made for a long workday. I got tired and the barn smells aggravated my allergies. In back of the barn there was a half-acre of tilled soil where in the spring potatoes, corn, and beans were planted, kept free of weeds throughout the summer, and harvested in the fall. All twelve youths got involved in this. When the day's work was done and the others went back into the house, Paula and I huddled in the lee of a shed and smoked our stolen tobacco while trying to piece together a plan for the future: when we would be old enough to get away, how we would get the money, where we would go. Our cigarette smoke mixed with the smell of boiled cabbage, the open slop hole, and the three-seat, wood chimney backhouse. These odours were like birthmarks in that they were steeped into our clothes so we could not smell them or wash them off. But our schoolteacher at St. Paul's told us we smelled like a rag barrel.

Even now, if I were blindfolded and taken there, I know a hurt would return with the scent of that place. There was a lot of rot at the home, one that mixed with the feelings of rejection and loneliness, a longing for something we did not understand and so could not describe. Often I contemplated, especially toward evening, the loneliest part of the day, the advantages of living on a farm or in a town house with conventional parents.

"I took his money, that's where I made my first mistake," Paula said, and turned her back to me as if she were ashamed. "I did it for fifty cents!"

"But you were only eleven years old!"

"The first time, yes."

"You felt you had to do it or be kicked out of the house."

"At first it was kissing, like a family was supposed to do, he said. How would I know what a family was supposed to do? Then he wanted the other and gave me a scarf and mittens, which I never wore. It didn't seem right wearing them because of how I got them."

"You would have done anything to be accepted."

It made me mad to think that Paula was so desperate for compassion that she did not fight him off. I was lonely too, of course I was. (No one ever lied about being lonely.) So I hugged her for a long time. I understood where she was coming from, that's for sure.

"What choice do I have right now but to keep on doing ...?"

"Not much. And Hayward knows you tell me things too."

"He hates you because of me and what you know," she said.

"I also peed in his whisky."

"David, you have to promise me that no matter how low you get, you won't do what your mother did – you know, with the rope. Now promise!"

"Paula, you know I can't promise that. When we are

in that state of mind we have no control over what we do.
Father Breau told me so the day Mum was buried."

"Then will you come to me if you get low?"

"I will, yes I will."

Paula turned and walked toward the river. I wanted
to follow but knew better. When she took off like that
without speaking, I knew she wanted to be alone.

I hollered, "Paula! We still have all our shit together,
don't we?"

She did not answer. How I longed for her at such
times.

Sometimes, I found her down on the river ice,
scuffing along, puffing on a cigarette. If she saw me and
turned her back, I knew I was not supposed to go near
her. But if she waved, I guessed it was okay to go to her. It
was as if she had times of deep thought and did not want
anyone around her. And then there were times when she
wanted me to be there. In either case there was always an
underlying sadness to our predicament.

When I was really low, I could understand why
Paula did what she did for Hayward, though I could not
stand him. I guess in some ways she was more desperate
than me. She prayed to be adopted by a caring family. And
I knew it was selfish of me, but I prayed that she would
stay at the Home. How could I live there without her?

Once in a while, a foster parent came by, looking
to adopt a child. They would sit in the office, talk to
Hayward, read the register, and look at photographs
before walking through the visiting room where, after
being scrubbed and dressed, we were stood in a row. I
never got lucky at these, and once I overheard a woman

tell Maria that I had troublesome eyes. I would go back to my room, heartbroken, yet glad that Paula was also rejected. There was a certain comfort in having someone to share rejection with. This worked for Paula also. To avoid disappointment, we learned to steal away at the sight of a prospective parent. Or if we were caught there, we acted like scamps.

Sometimes, when Maria was out shopping, Paula and I went to her room to pose in front of her big burlesque mirror. We made stern faces like those in antique photographs. From Maria's carnival days – she was a Mexican who had come to town with the Bill Lynch Show – she had hats with long feathers, fancy umbrellas, bloomers that sparkled, and garters trimmed with black lace that made Paula look like a dance hall girl. She would sashay around the room before crowding beside me on the circus trunk that fronted the looking glass. Paula had the most beautiful eyes I ever saw. They were so moist that when she lowered her long lashes it was like someone had closed the curtains on a window.

Sometimes when Hayward was out, I sat at his desk with two or three orphans in front of me and told the radio news. Using a table spoon for a microphone, I was Lorne Greene, who came to us through CBC Radio. I learned how to exaggerate my voice, deep and low to make the news funny. Once I was Dick Tracy with a wristwatch I talked into and answered myself in the voice of Edgar Bergen, a ventriloquist I had heard on the radio. I could also juggle three oranges without dropping one. You could say that my need to get away got me away from there spiritually.

"Happiness is in the mind, not the place," Maria said to Hayward when he caught me at his desk. "His imagination is more active than the others. Because of the medications he has taken for polio, he is overly sensitive."

One Sunday a young boy from Ben's Settlement was dropped off at the youth home, his mother having been killed in a car accident. Sandy Hunter did not want to stay and there was a great tussle with his father. When Mr. Hunter drove away, Sandy ran after his car for a long way up the road. He was calling, "Daddy, Daddy, please don't leave me here alone. I don't want to stay here without you!"

And the sound of the boy's voice pleading with his father brought tears to my eyes, even though I had heard it by others many times.

I can still hear the desperate screaming, "Daddy! Daddy, don't go! Please don't go and leave me here alone." But the car moved on without his father looking back. Sandy, in his little tweed cap and britches, sat on the doorstep beside his cardboard suitcase and sobbed. Maria came out and took him into the house and tried to get him to eat. But he refused the food. He would not speak to any of us for months, and every Sunday afternoon, for two years, he got dressed in his best clothes, sat on the front steps with the little suitcase, and waited for his father to come and take him back to their home. But he never came. Until through time, Sandy eventually became one of us. "You can't be more alone than when you are with the wrong people," he told me. "I don't know where he is but he knows where I am. So if he wanted to see me he could drop by." Already, he had that eternal sadness in his young eyes. "But I will find him someday. We have the same name."

We all waited for one of our relatives to come and visit, especially on the parents' visitation days. But we never saw them. Until we were tired of waiting and wrote them off as lost family. They were the ones lost, not us. They knew where *we* were.

One day Hayward told us that if we got the fall's work done early, we would get a visit from singing cowboy Gene Autry, who was coming to an orphans' home in Saint John. For a month Paula and I followed every rule. We stacked the firewood, knelt by our beds for the prayers at night, and stood by the organ with the others to sing "The Empire Is Our Home." But my hero did not come. And I never believed anything Hayward told me after that.

Sometimes we got a surprise visit from inspectors of the Children's Aid Society, at other times the Canadian Welfare Council. These men in dark suits and women in pleated skirts – they came in one big car and gave each of us a sucker – told us we had to keep ourselves clean and stay out of trouble. "Get involved in sports," they said. "Play hopscotch, play baseball."

Once a month, the Youth Home Committee held a meeting in the visiting room. Before these gatherings, Hayward told us we had to keep our mouths shut. So while they were in the house we spoke to no one except to him or Maria.

Sometimes The Board of Trustees invited visitors to the Home on a day of "open house." This was an attempt to raise money for the cause. The children entertained; some of the kids displayed their model cars, air planes, or handiwork. One kid built a model farm, complete with wooden horses and cows, like his old home near Smith Falls had been. He kept telling visitors he wanted to go back there to live when he grew up. Paula played the organ and sang "The Ballad of a Teenage Queen" and got a clap of hands. Using a wool sock for a dummy I talked with my mouth closed in the voices of Edgar Bergen and Charlie McCarthy. Everyone clapped and whistled. I took a bow. It was a nice feeling to be appreciated by adults and I wanted to do more, but Hayward, who wouldn't know shit from applesauce, said my show was over and pushed me off the stage.

One day when Maria was shopping and Hayward was deer hunting I went upstairs to find Paula in her bed reading. She did not wave me away so I crawled in beside her. When she touched my private parts the sound of my heart beating filled the room and I became fevered with a new-found hunger. This was mixed with a strong surge of hatred and jealousy toward Hayward for what he was doing to the woman I loved. It was a sweet delight all mixed up with bitterness, like candy doused in boric acid. But the candy prevailed.

We were making out when the door opened and Maria was standing with a broom in her hand. She shouted and started swinging, breaking the broom handle over my back as I ran across the hall. In my room I stood against the door. My back was smarting.

That evening Maria did not fix supper for me, and I was so hungry. But toward bedtime, Paula sneaked upstairs with a few cookies. I was afraid there would be a beating when Hayward came home. But the incident was never mentioned; I guessed Maria never told him. But her cold stares made me feel guilty for sitting at the table to eat with the others. They all knew I loved Paula, but that I did not really possess her.

From that time on, Maria made Paula do more than her share of house chores. I supposed she felt my lover was also to blame. Paula scrubbed floors and carried the chamber pails through deep snow, emptying them down a hole in the backhouse. The clothes that we hung on the line froze into stiff carcasses that Paula dragged into the kitchen to stand behind the stove before ironing. To help Paula, each morning I made beds before going to school.

When Paula was fifteen she got pregnant. Of course Maria blamed it on me. She told Paula she was going to tell the Children's Foundation Committee she caught me in bed with her and that I would spend time behind bars. This worried me so I could not do my school work, until Paula went to her and said I had not done it.

I figured it was Hayward. He stalked us in the wee hours when we were in a sound sleep. There was a certain mystery about those things, a mental block that kept us from going there afterwards, as if it had happened in a dream. I guessed we were afraid a scandal would leave us homeless. I asked myself, "Where could we go?"

Maria gave Paula a gypsy potion from roots of herbs and a good dose of castor oil. When the fetus was born, it was buried in the night, behind the house, under a tree with a rock for a marker. Only Maria and Paula knew where, though I saw it from a distance.

When they returned, I wrapped my arms around Paula and could feel her heart beating, like when you hold a bird that has a broken wing.

For sure the Youth Home was a rugged place to grow up, though people have told me I have no scars.

Not like Paula McKenzie, who wears the pot-hook bangs to hide the X on her forehead that turns purple because she is out in the cold.

Undercurrents

Feeling the warmth of the river wind on our freckled faces, and with our shadows racing before us, we made our way toward the Sand Bar, with Colleen walking ahead of me, her bare feet untanned. We had been high school sweethearts for almost two years and had done many things together, excluding sex of course, because we were too young, and also of different religions, which would have prevented us from marrying in any circumstance. Plus many teens from our school had gotten pregnant and ended up marrying for the wrong reasons.

We had also been warned, by teachers and parents, not to go to this place to swim as there was an undertow that was said to be thirty feet deep. Many people had drowned here, including two of Colleen's uncles in the old days, and just five years before, Gerry White, a friend from my class – he had great potential – had been dragged down. I could remember watching from the opposite side of the river and seeing the rescue people with the grappling hooks raking the river bottom, while Gerry's mother stood on the shore with prayer beads, going over the Rosary. The boy's father, a sickly-looking man, stood in gloomy silence, staring into the water as the big hooks brought up pieces of Gerry's swimsuit.

I wondered which was the most difficult to deal with: watching your drowned son's body, faded and limp, being pulled from the undertow or seeing your father die on the ground, having been kicked in the chest by a Clydesdale at the horse hauling contest at the village fairgrounds. (My mother and I wore black clothing for a long time after that day.)

Now, in spite of the ghosts, Colleen and I walked across the bridge. And the sun cast our dancing shadows against the plank railings. We made our way along the towpath that followed the riverbank and were drawn out onto the hot sand, where we took off our shirts and lay down on a beach towel to get a suntan. Colleen, the lady in pink of my adolescence, was wearing a red, two-piece bathing suit and her curly black hair glistened under the sheen of the sun, her teeth white as ivory, her smile creating dimples. I wore the only swimwear I owned: cut-off blue jeans and worn-out canvas sneakers.

"You know that we are rebels because of our coming here," I said.

"I love you," she said and kissed me.

"I love you more."

On one another's backs, thighs, and calves we rubbed tanning lotions that made our skin glisten under the shimmer of the sun. It was very hot and the blossom-and-fish-scented water was inviting, but we resisted the temptation to wade into the shallows as neither of us could swim that well and we feared the undercurrents. We had brought Cokes and chips we picked up at Mack's Diner over in the village and intended to stay all afternoon, having planned this day for a long time. It would be a break from our routine of schoolroom and home chores with indolence being our worst flaw for the day. The morning was pleasant and agreeable, the only sounds being that of water bubbling around the foot of an island just upstream – salmon were jumping there – and truck tires that howled on the paved highway, Main Street, in Falconer across the river. Also on the opposite riverbank, a trolley puttered down the railway and its occupants waved at us.

Colleen and I had just finished our school year, had gone to the junior prom together, and were free for the time being, although we both had summer jobs to go to at the end of June. She would work at Jack's Grocery in Swing Town as she had done for two years, and I on the pulp truck of Tom Hennessy, where we would take two loads of boxwood to the sawmills in town each day. This would not be an easy task for me as Tom's truck had no hydraulic lift and the logs had to be pushed up on the load by hand. Still, it was a summer job and I was glad to have it. I can remember working on the truck the summer before and how tiring it was, and how all my thoughts were of Colleen, a young woman who had an eye for paintings, an ear for good music, and the heart for a good book.

To the prom Colleen had worn a simple lawn dress, open sandals, and a cluster of potato blossom that I had given her for a corsage. I wore a white shirt without a necktie, a turned-up collar, and with the sleeves rolled up to my elbows. We danced all evening and then I took her home in a car I had hired at Jack's Diner. Because I had no money left, I walked to my own home, which was four miles up the gravel highway from the village. It was at the dance that we planned this day together.

Now as we lay side by side, facing the sun, Colleen's big brown eyes were closed so tightly that the meeting lashes were seen as one. But when she opened them they were as wide as the sky, dreamy and all-consuming. I turned to give her a kiss and when our lips touched, I could taste her sunscreen lotion and the Coke and potato chips that were in her teeth. We kissed long and deep and I could feel her arms caressing my back. We rolled together on the beach towel in an uncompromising embrace, tugging at one another's swimsuits to get them off and puffing like a bellows. Our love for one another, a hunger to try mature things, and the passion that oozed from our hormones prevailed. We were both on fire so there was no resistance, either way, no foreplay whisky needed. After exploring each other's bodies we made love on the towel, spread on the hot Sand Bar in the middle of the day, with only a perfumed lilac bush sheltering us from view of the highway. It was the first time for each of us and while it was heated and, oh so fanatical, we were nervous, her appearing more so than I. But having come from a broken family, it was really beautiful for me to be loved to this degree.

Afterwards, with an air of indifference, Colleen turned her back to me, as if something earth-shattering had befallen her. And I was sorry that I had let our lovemaking happen so easily. I felt that I had abused her, that she had trusted me to not go too far, and that I had let her down. I was two years older than Colleen and probably could have swung it around, mid-stream. But heated embraces, exploring kisses, and hormones have no conscience. And here now, relaxed, though guilt-ridden, it was easy to look back and see my weakness; an act which occurred in the heat of the moment, but in truth, an experience I had been looking forward to all my young life, wondering if real lovemaking would live up to the fantasies I had so often experienced in dreams. It had been all of that and more. For a brief instant I felt like a sentimentalist with no illusions left to pursue, a criminal who had pushed his luck too far and was now on the wanted list. And my mind hovered between my earlier imaginings and the experience itself. Had the pleasure, so brief, been worth it?

But like the Sand Bar, which we were warned against going to, something had also drawn us to do the sex, a thing that each of us wanted and had unconsciously planned for a long time, something we had also been warned against. It was like everyone – parents, teachers, the minister, the nuns, and the churches – were in defiance of both these new experiences, and I believe that the attempt to control us was what pushed us to do it. Those old-school teachings appeared to be filled with images of people who were no longer capable of loving anyone, even themselves, all their successive lives, their hearts having saddened to coincide with their hard-core faces, their faculties no longer aware of the distance between the two. This was a very real fear when we were young, as was the dishonour in having disobeyed.

"I feel so ashamed right now," Colleen said. And she cried like a child. Well, she was a child at heart. Suddenly the sun, the sand, and the river were invisible and a dark cloud had taken over the day so that the sky was the gray of an old handsaw. We were both feeling guilt, having been preached to, having been told by authorities that to disobey was certainly a sin and that sex was a bigger sin. And I felt like trash for not only letting it happen, but undeniably leading her into it. We waded into the shallows and scrubbed one another from head to toe, and then we went back to lie on the towel. But guilt was a thing that the water would not wash away. And the towel, sand, and sun offered none of their former attractions. Indeed, clouds had gathered in the heavens.

"I feel like a proper tramp," Colleen said with tears in her words.

"I love you very much," I said. "It was true lovemaking, nothing more."

"Then why do I feel ..."

"Colleen, I'm so sorry."

"I didn't want it to be *this* way. Not on the shore of the river."

"Then why did we come here?" I said with a friendly note.

I put a hand on her forehead and she appeared to have a fever, or maybe it was just the effects of the sun and these new-found emotions. She put an index finger on my lips. "No, please don't! Don't touch me, not right now. I have to sort all this out in my head."

I was sensible to the fact that she was in great despair, but it saddened me to think that I could not touch someone who to me was the most beautiful person in the world. It was like I had committed an act of trespass; that to her the sight of me just then brought back something that should have never happened. And I felt like I had taken advantage and that I was some kind of abuser, even a sex predator. Knowing her good breeding, her childlike good manners, and the kindness of her heart, I felt that she was trying to cover her emotions, draw within herself, shield this new state of mind from me as much as possible, but it was obvious that she was deeply troubled.

For me, our togetherness at this point was more about healing, of reassuring each other that what we had done was not a crime, though perhaps immoral. Colleen was a young Christian woman with unimpeachable moral conduct, someone who was obviously tired of the virtuous life and secretly wanted to explore new adventures, while not thinking of the after effects and now appeared to be longing for solitude. She felt uncomfortable with me and vexed that I had taken that old happy innocence from her. But for my part, I felt the sex would help us blend together into the most sacred and loving ties of life.

At length she said, "Please don't tell your friends about any of this, will you?"

"Not a chance," I said. "No one has to know what happened at the Sand Bar. And if you never want to see me again, I'll understand."

"I just want to go home," she said. She was sitting in the lotus position and staring into the water. And while she had not yet left me, I felt like I was already alone.

Silently, even unconsciously, we got up, gathered our things and walked down the shore and made our way across the bridge – its floor planking echoed hollow sounds when a car went past us – and on up to Main Street where we sat, not speaking, on the steps of the Public Dance Hall.

As we walked, I noticed that she kept her face turned away from me. We had become two islands, two troubled minds, well contained, each battling our own demons. And even though I really wanted to give her a hug, I made a point not to touch her. She had become a closed book to me, indifferent and motionless as a sphinx. It was like we were both afraid, her more so than me, and for different reasons, as if each one was secretly blaming the other for what we had done. But I was more concerned about losing her as a lover than any of the other things the sex had set spinning in our heads. It was an afternoon that had become all tangled up with issues that were immoral and sad. And even now the sight of the bridge and the Public Hall still takes me back to that old Sand Bar state of mind.

Colleen said finally that she would have to keep this secret from her folks, go to confession as soon as possible, talk to a priest, and clean up her self-deprecatory thoughts, the guilt and the self-blame she was experiencing, so much greater now than any desire she had had to have done the sex, before her life could go back to normal, if ever. Because she knew the sin could never really be undone and that she was no longer pure. But to me these were things that appeared to skate right over what was really deep in her heart.

I was worried too, but for different reasons. What if she had gotten pregnant? There was something about pregnancy that I was afraid of, especially after my mother had a miscarriage and lost her baby on a Halloween night ten years before, when Daddy was alive, and had almost hemorrhaged to death. (She had been in the hospital for two months.) These are things you do not think about when you are in love and hungry for sex. But I knew too that if Colleen was really expecting a baby, I would trade my mother and surrogate father for a wife, join her church regardless of what my parents thought, see that she got through it safely, support her and the child, and try to make us a good family, to be together forever, which was something I had dreamed of but not experienced this far in life.

But I also knew, down deep, that for her, and her family's sake, she needed to meet someone better than me, and that I was not good enough for her. I felt she had been naive, had lived a sheltered life and needed to travel a bit before she decided on a man to accompany her through life. And that was where my real guilt came from. She deserved a man who was not working on a pulp truck for wages, rather someone who was employed in a bank in town and well-to-do, a "somebody." She needed someone who could take her up the scale, give her freedom to pursue her own dreams and not drag her down, to my level. I also knew that whatever happened, I would never have sex with her again. As soon as we found out for certain that she was *not* pregnant, whether she liked it or not, I would break up with her, so she could move on, find someone more deserving of her, though I knew it would be very painful for me, because she was the only woman I would ever love, even to this day. For sure I would be a bachelor for life.

When at her front door, I tried to kiss her cheek, she turned away and put her hands in her jean pockets, I assumed to keep from hugging me. I felt that I would not see her for a long time if ever, but I was hoping that her former kindness would prevail and leave me with a lasting and peaceful impression, something I could take home with me as a token of spiritual value and not a memory that was messed up with anxiety and dejection. But I would rather not see her again than have her suffer at the sight of me.

On the streets in Falconer, or in Ben's Grocery Store where we sometimes met, she would speak politely and then move on quickly without stopping to chat. I was really saddened at her show of disinterestedness. Each time this happened I was wounded. What I suffered alone was nothing, but the thought that *she* was distressed saddened me. I knew she was tormented because of her silence. I had read in *The Times* that when someone is ignoring you, they are troubled and not really ignoring you at all, but instead are trying to deal with things inside themselves. I now believe that we live in ignorance of those we love. And I wondered if she could see who I was more clearly than I could see myself. Or perhaps she could not see clearly who I was, who she was. Whatever it was, my mind was filled with a first romance, sex, and then heartbreak.

Twice I wrote a letter – mailing them to her address on the Browne Road, telling her that I loved her very much, that I was really hurting, and that I wanted to be back into her life, not in a sexual way, but as before in a platonic fashion. But she never answered my pleas or acknowledged that she even received them. And there were times when I never slept a wink for a whole week. Still, I was hoping that with time, and prayer, she might let me back into her world.

It was at this time that I learned from an old friend

that she had been seen hanging out with a prominent young woman from town; that they had been spotted sitting in the Village Diner together, holding hands, as women will, as if to comfort one another. And suddenly I could understand her indifference toward me. And for some reason, I was not jealous. Instead I was pleased that she had met someone intelligent, a person she could grow up to. And I said to myself, "Good for you, Colleen, you have met someone deserving of your love." I knew that she was better off without me in her life, and that for her long-term well-being, I had nothing to offer but melancholy and transience. While I loved myself, I loved her more, valued her more as a person of the mind, and I knew I would love her when I no longer loved myself. I would miss the physical closeness but not the spiritual, as I had never experienced much of this anyway, as I said, having come from a broken home. It was then I stopped looking for her. I was thinking that if I never saw her again, it would be easier for us both, though I knew she would always be present in my heart, just the way she was that morning at the Sand Bar.

When she finally made contact with me through a letter, saying that she wanted to meet with me, I did not answer because I had already suffered her loss, having shouldered the wounds of a broken heart and had now healed somewhat. Owing to the fact that I knew she was by this time with a new love, someone of her own persuasion, and was better off, I needed to make this sacrifice for her, and perhaps avoid the embarrassment of having her try to explain to me the reasons for her indifference. So in that sense, by this time I had been neglecting her. But I felt that having suffered her loss, I had to be strong and let her go.

So in August when I got the news that Colleen had drowned at the Sand Bar, that she had gone there alone to swim during dog-days and was dragged down by the undercurrents, I was shocked. I wondered what I might have done differently. Should I have kept pursuing her? I don't think so. Should I have been more forceful and less divisive in my actions? Should I have given up the ghost, long before? Should I have met with her? I also wondered if she had secretly found out that she was pregnant, or if she was a woman who loved only other women. But of course I had no way of knowing what was going on inside her head. Or was it simply because she had lost her virginity, lost her innocence and her morality, to someone of the wrong religion, a narrow-minded country lad she could never really love long term?

Everyone in the village was baffled as to why the young woman with so much promise had gone to that forsaken place alone, it being such an alluring but dangerous swimming hole, her being so responsible. This beautiful young woman with the whole world at her feet had suddenly gotten caught up in undercurrents that were fathoms deep.

And I was lonesome as hell for my old love.

River Love

This is the moment I have been waiting for. On this brilliant June morning, as I wade into the cool river, there are petals adrift from the cherry blossoms, exclamation marks in an early summer of prose. And there is a film of pollen on the water that has been changing slowly from a single-malt Scotch to vodka that has been distilled by the years; the rocky bottom where the pinfish dart is gray and sparkling. (There would be small pieces of gold and silver in that gravel, I think.)

I am listening to the voice of birds, the gurgle of the water while I cast the double-tapered fly-line I have received as a Christmas gift. Like the first golf swing of the season, at this point the fundamentals of the long cast are held together by the continuity of habit. Since my imaginative boyhood I have been in love with this old river, her most endearing impressions having been printed forever in my memory. I grasp for the stream's subtle spirit, the myth, the superiority of soul and her reaching arms. My addiction to this water is like that of the smoke of a good cigar. As it flows in and around me, it turns my bones into jelly and makes me weak at the knees. In its tastes and scents, I can see my depleting bank account grow larger, my humble river home expand into a castle, my muse beckon with new ideas for a poem, my depravity of love into a thousand wanton and comely women. I am protective in disallowing any omens to the contrary. Ah, yes, the fix of a good river.

Around me, the hills and gullies are also cheerful within themselves. They are filled with nodding dandelions, cattle grazing contentedly, the brook on the other side chatting like so many conspiring elves. The clement sky brings forth the shadows of hillside trees to reflect on the water in shades of green, as I have seen the moon, on frosty winter nights, turn the whole concern into silver. This place of exile requires no human embroidery. I have always needed more space than most – distance and time to be alone. I am bored in small, idle groups and their small talk. The river is a place for spiritual healing. That is why, so it seems to me, this kind of exile is the best location to be in during the isolation periods brought on by the COVID-19 pandemic. There is nowhere else I would rather be on this still, early-summer's day.

Up on the hill in my summer kitchen – I have "moved out" just two weeks ago – the wood range is smoking with crumbs from the morning's toast and there is the scent of pitch from the green wood drying in the oven. There is also a sour smell from the linoleum-covered washstand that has a slop pail below the hole that supports the dish pan. A breeze whispers through the screen door that is held shut by a coiled spring. And beside the woodshed there are burnt tea leaves – dumped there through the winter – that nourish the carrot-scented caraway already in blossom. These are the seasonal smells of my old river home, a place where the electronic age has never really penetrated.

Early this morning, on my way to the pool, a pleasant old man – he is a retired Anglican priest who is religious but not obsessively so – wearing a black wig and monk sandals tugged my sleeve and, in a serious tone of voice, told me there were bright salmon in the river, although, he says, he has not seen one as yet.

Misting his breath upon his spectacles and wiping them clean with a handkerchief, he talked on. "Everything here springs from chance. An early June fish will seldom break water; they are like ghosts. They rarely hold up; rather they travel in small schools of two or three as they advance to the headwaters while the river is still cold and deep. So the probability of hooking this fish is hit-and-miss, like dancing with a giraffe," he said with a chuckle. "When I was a youngster, at this time of year, I anchored my canoe in the middle of the river and cast from side to side. I was hoping a Rocky Brooker would swim under the moving fly-hook. Those big salmon, fresh from the sea, would most always raise and take the hook. The first one of the season was the most exciting, the first of one's life, more still. We were never really certain that these fish were in the river until we actually hooked one. So there was an element of mystery around the place. But it was my affection for the river and the great fish that brought me here so often. There is love in all things here: the people, the trees, the fish, and the water itself."

"We are river pilgrims," I told him.

"Yes, we are pilgrims," the old man said and I could

hear him wheezing as he left the river and walked back to his car.

I remember the patriarch's words and observe the dimples in the big slow-moving river. Indeed, the first sightings are the most dramatic. And a wake or a boil does not account for much because they could be made by gaspereau or shad. (These coarse fish will sometimes take a salmon fly-hook too.) But I know this water and the music it will make if fished properly. Yet, when it comes to the Atlantic salmon, I still have a lot to learn. So much so that, for me, the great river has become a wildlife conservatory, a place wherein I need practice in finding her colour tones, her delicate flat and sharp movements. I cast and wait for the big pull from below, the long run downstream, the high jump which will tug my heartstrings and irrevocably leave no doubt in my mind as to what fish it is.

Treacherously sentimental, I now believe that the heart is the only accurate witness in this pilgrimage, in the way that love is really God, and that one covets only what one cannot possess. Like a true love, a river is remote, difficult to attain, but once captured, harder to let go of. (This is not my first rodeo, not my primary encounter with divinity, the noble Atlantic salmon. And like this game fish, I now believe that a woman's seclusion, because she has kept a man in a state of waiting, will serve only to magnify his unrelenting persuasion to bring her into his arms.) In the words of Marcel Proust, "Love is space and time made perceptible to the heart."

Suddenly I realize that it is not about the fish so much but the fishing that I am here for, not about love but the pursuit of love. Adoration is harder found but longer lasting, which is the way of all good romances, all good salmon rivers. As I cast and wait, I stare into the water for a glimpse, by virtue of which I can measure the emotions. I follow the movement of the leader and fly-hook while it tracks across the flow at a seventy-five-degree angle. In a daze, this is a fixed stare, like that of the Queen of Hearts. The cast is straight, without a curve or a wrinkle as it swings like the pendulum on a grandfather clock. The river is also therapeutic, I think. It lifts me out of mediocrity; it is an anti-depressant for any state of mind: anger, disdain, pandemic relief, short-sightedness, lack of confidence, and a host of other emotional ailments.

Each outing is like experiencing the excitement of a first date. Like youth and love time, each fish hooked, each pull from below, is an orgasm.

To tell the truth, sometimes I think it is the things I most desire to which I pretend to attach the least importance. I keep this all inside myself like the incomplete recollections and meditations of Horace or Virgil. I hold myself against the heavy currents, cast in an orthodox way, using the early-summer fly-hook of white goat hair I have tied last winter. In my melancholy thoughts, from those long-past morning-less nights, it is like I have forgotten what an Atlantic salmon actually looks and feels like, because I have exaggerated its likeness and speed tenfold in so many winter dreams. Such is the falsehood of memory.

On winter nights, sleeping by my fireside, I dream of the great waters and those huckleberry river days. And like a city spire that tolls the passing of an elder, the big clock on the mantel hammers out the hours, old time, slow time, my time. In the chimney's voices there is the threat of snow.

Still, there is nowhere else I would rather be. The miles separate me from town in the physical and moral sense. Like the naturalist and isolationist Henry David Thoreau, I do not want to go there. Why leave an academy that is filled with nature and youthful promise? Why leave these fields of wonder to tread upon city sidewalks, intellect be damned? There is never a lonesome sunset here, no old English silver, no straw men to burn in effigy.

Long ago when I was a schoolboy, on winter evenings, my friends and I played hockey. In those river games, for sticks we used the branches of crooked alder and for a puck, the heel of a discarded shoe. From the middle of the river we could see, along the far shore, the protruding leafless dogwood that looked like so many charcoal sketches, the black trees beyond. And in the beaver meadows there were ragged cattails that stood like shotgun cleaners, the snow blue under the trees that moaned like an unresting sorrow.

Beneath a twinkling galaxy, we built bonfires that lit up the river for a long way, the silent water below. We stood in a circle and roasted wieners that were held over the flame on green saplings, our faces red from frostbite. For us boys it was not cool to wear caps; rather we used the skin-coloured hems of our mother's nylon stockings to keep our ears from freezing. But the girls enjoyed a certain vogue with their long scarves and stocking-leg caps with tassels that hung down the side. These wraps trailed off in the breeze as they skated beside us along that endless windblown rink between Taylor's Mountain and Keenan's wire bridge. Of course an artist is always more sensitive to such encounters, such memories, which at my age are now fading, as a dream fades. Old bones and old hearts get careworn at this time in life. It is all so long ago, there are times when I think it all might have happened to someone else.

Sickly as a boy, I can remember hooking my first salmon in these waters when I was eight years old, my second memory in life. The fish's long run downstream made the line burn my fingers. For a while, I felt like the strength of that great fish was my very own – until it jumped, shook its head, and went free. That big salmon was never as mighty in its short presence as it is now in reminiscence. It has become impregnated with my spirit, yet it remains original.

There has been no salmon this morning, no music, no heart throbs to amplify the river's soul. But the great game fish, or the allusions of fish, has played a role in keeping my time filled with the possibility of what an early summer morning can bring.

September Mourning

It had been a cool night. I should have closed the front door. My sleep is disturbed by the sharp staccato whistle of the osprey. I turn in my bed, experiencing the mingling and melting away of night dreams. Half-conscious, I can hear a pulp truck on the distant chip-seal road. That would be my friend Donny Brophy going to work. He is a trucker who lives just up the highway in what used to be my uncle's farmhouse. There is a gray dawn at the window, a late summer chill.

You lie beside me with your face to the wall. I put an arm about your waist and pull you to me, knowing that tonight I will be alone in this bed, scenting your perfume on the pillow, reliving this summer of loving you. And trying to justify letting you go without a struggle. Tomorrow, I think, learning how to live alone begins again. But now there is calm and I lay and wait for the osprey's territorial signal but hear only the gurgle of the brook nearby and the buzz of a housefly in the lighted bathroom.

I get up and stagger to the bathroom, have a drink of water, then I go to the screened door to look at the river. Subtle, ever so subtle waves move out across the water from the brook's mouth where the salmon are lying in the colder water. The river itself is warm, low and clear. I can smell its bottom along the shores where the water has dropped: decaying algae, sun-baked stones, clam shells, life jackets, and sweaty sneakers. There are junks of foam adrift in the channel. They crowd together in the run like lemmings. Later they will make moving shadows against the amber bottom before burning off as the sun strengthens.

Higher along the opposite shore is the dewed meadow grass, tall and silent, now showing a few strands of yellow. The grassy hillside beyond is yellow with wildflowers. The trees, double green, are now tinted slightly. And beyond the foliage, the lofty pink sky. Everything is tranquil, even holy, the way that Sunday's drive home from church used to be from the back seat of my father's car when I was a child. In my mind I try two cadenzas in the scene. First Pachelbel's *Canon in D*, then J.S. Bach's *Gavotte in D Major*. These do not do justice to the morning, and I block them out, let my senses overrule my intellect. Then the little brook rises up to sing, chuckle, gurgle, gulp. This is the better score, I think.

I stand behind the screen door in my shorts and T-shirt. No breeze yet, not a whisper. The grass in the yard is silver with dew. The boardwalk to the woodshed is silver, as is my car windshield. And now a raven whoops, some kind of warning, I suspect. Or maybe it is trying to out-sing the brook (as I did a few moments ago). A red squirrel runs from limb to limb in the trees that hug our cabin. It stops to scold at my presence in the doorway. And I realize, only now, that I do not have the senses keen enough to see and feel the whole picture in the way of the raven and the squirrel. But of course I love it just as much. This place is all I know, because, you see, I have never been away. Not even for the winter like the osprey or the crane. And because this is my whole life, I now take some comfort in the fact that this is not a rainy day. Rain, I think, would bring down a power failure right now.

I look into the bedroom where you are sleeping. Only your face is exposed above the covers. Your long lashes are pretty upon faded summer cheeks. Pretty lashes that hide dark passionate eyes, full of thought, full of love, revealing your feelings long before you say a word. You think these parts of you are nothing, but I know them to be the nothingness of greatness.

In your eyes too are the lingering images of a daddy's little girl, freckled and skinny with twisted sandals, denim jeans, ball cap, and the sunglasses you found in the river. You have been queen of the junior prom, valedictorian on graduation day. You have been your mother's loyal daughter too, postured with earrings, pantyhose, a touch of makeup, but always keeping that awkward smile that is real and the youthful spirit. Even with me you have been crazy and funny, mature and graceful, tomboyish, a fishing partner for years, a true love with eyes that drew me to them with a moisture so rich and deep that whoever you looked at fell in love with you. I think of our years together. You and I on the river: canoeing, barbecuing, skating, and this old cabin. I see you in a meditative pose, reclining on the wood bench under our pine tree. I see you in wading boots, casting a fly-line with the grace of a ballet dancer. I wish I could do it all again, but only with you.

Now, all of the years are suddenly condensed into two small images. Our old boat is under sail and you are standing at the back with both hands on the rudder bar, your slim bathing-suited body braced against the rail, hair stringy, shrill voice singing (after just one beer) a sea shanty you hardly even know. You ad-lib the words and make some up. You are trying to impress me. This is followed by a comfort in the way you embrace me when I am down. These images come together now, embracing and singing, embracing and singing. They dance like ghosts in a morning fog.

You will be leaving today, to go to the University of Toronto. This is your chance to grow, get sophisticated. This is your chance to become a *somebody*. When you come back you will be another Catharine. You will have set aside your local river dialect, your corny humour, your homely innocent warmth, that spring spirit. In a sense you will never return. Not really. Not the way you are. Changes, new information will have made you ashamed of who you are and where you come from. Ideas will govern your spirit and refine your posture so that you will stay always and irreversibly within their boundaries, not yours. And not mine.

Later this morning I will kiss you goodbye and try not to show emotion, not even a hint of melancholy as you drive away. Sad to see you go but knowing it would be sadder if you were content to stay. I would feel guilty for standing in your way. Because I realize now I cannot help you through tomorrow. I have no more nourishment, no new philosophic direction in which to lead you. You might say that I have been your April man, a spectator who has watched you grow beyond me, watched you pine and suffer within yourself because you did so, though you have always loved me for the man I am. Now, the most important thing to me is that you keep growing to make this hurt worth something. I could ask you to stay for my own selfish reasons because I know you love me enough to do it. Maybe you do. But I cannot stand still and watch you become me. Not for a minute. And you would. I guarantee.

So I sit at my computer to write this secret note to you while you are still sleeping and before the day gets hot. I will put this in your suitcase, there in the back pocket where your writing paper and family photos are. You will read it in your room in Toronto someday down the road and think of me with that goodness of yours. I hope. Somewhere on the river, in the same instant, I will think of you. And I will remember you just the way you are this morning.

The Cains

(A River of Broken Promise)

As I went down to the river to pray,
Studyin' 'bout that good ol' way ...
Oh, brothers, let's go down, come on down,
Don't you wanna go down.
Down to the river to pray.

~ Traditional American Folksong,
Anonymous

My family used to think that the Cains was our river, that we had a special empathy with its woods and waters and that its ancestral kinship was a big part of our family posterity. But then we learned that millions of other families, once they experienced its seductiveness, claimed and loved it also.

On a Sunday morning in October, having left my Miramichi cabin at dawn, we drove in the rain for fifteen miles up the Mill Road to where we turned off and parked in a grassy area at the top of the Cold Brook Hill. From there we followed a path to the old Buttermilk Brook log-landing site from where we could see for a long way up our river's biggest tributary, the Cains. Black as tar and infringed with orange grass, it made two bends before it came in close to the bottom of this high incline. Here was where my grandfather had once owned a log cabin. This was where on a December morning in '34, my father and grandfather were cooking breakfast when they heard the "clicking" of hooves. They went out onto the veranda and watched the last of the woodland caribou, one hundred and fifty strong, walking in a straight line – with a female in the lead – as they headed up the river ice. The beautiful, gray-bearded animals were migrating out of the province of New Brunswick, never to return. This was also where my father and his brothers, when they were youngsters, rode to on horseback Saturday mornings, spent the day shooting or fishing, stayed the night in Papa's camp, and rode back out on Sunday.

In my time, my brothers and I came in here on the back of my uncle Robert's '48 Dodge pickup with ponchos made of garbage bags to ward off the wind and rain. We fly-fished and hiked along those crooked log-driving trails. This was also where, during the river drive, someone on a landing rolled a log over this hill and my father, who was halfway up, saw it coming just in time to jump in the air as high as he could, so the log went under his feet, as if he had been skipping a rope. Indeed, it was a rugged place to work for a youngster who was out of school at the age of twelve.

On this morning, for nostalgic reasons, my cousin George – he worked in a bank in town – and I brought our fathers Charlie and Dan and our uncle Alex, all of whom had planned on fishing, but because of the rain and the cold wind had opted to cook. We had plenty of food and drinks for the day, which we carried in packsacks while treading upon the slippery, dead leaves and frost-killed bracken as we helped the older men over the hill. There was also mud on the trail that wound around the short-growth trees and the exposed roots, on down to the shore where cream-coloured water was coming out of the hillside and spilling over a ledge, Buttermilk Brook.

We set up camp on the riverbank in a grove of big, low-limbed spruce at the downriver end of the pool. (Those beautiful trees would be taken down the next February in an ice jam.) The old men built a fire on the ground and set out to make tea and cook for the party. They had found an old board door that had probably come adrift in the spring freshet and planned on using it for a table. The smell of the wet bracken was strong and there was a high cold wind that made the big trees sigh and toss about, their remaining leaves convulsing. Some of the maple foliage dropped in the water and, half-submerged, was carried away, red against black. Also on the intervale there was an old apple tree with clematis choking its trunk and with a few of last summer's apples clinging to its limbs. But these were too high up. I thought that this antiquated tree was symbolic of the river's livelihood in that there had been no low-hanging fruit, the opportunities for long-term survival well beyond reach.

George and I went to the top of the pool to start fishing down through the hundred-yard-long run in hopes of hooking some of those big brown salmon that we knew would be in the tea-stained waters at this time of year. As we fished through a silver mist of rain, we could see the blue smoke filtering out from among the tree branches, catch the sight of the orange flames that lapped around the fire logs, hear the animated laughter and singing, as in church – "In The Sweet By and By," "Softly and Tenderly Jesus is Calling," and "The Old Rugged Cross." The old men appeared to be pleased to be at this river on an autumn Sunday. (It could have been a Southern Baptist revival.) And even now so many years later, those hymns take me back to that place and time. When the damp winds shifted to come out of the northeast, to freeze my hands and make the river choppy, I could smell the pocketed fragrances of bacon frying and the homemade toast that was obviously burning on the grill. The smoke was catching in the breeze and puffing through the branches as if a bellows had been set pumping. I went to shore for a hot drink.

By then Uncle Alex had been given the nickname "Smoky," an affectionate diminutive, because he was doing the serious cooking and had smoke in his eye and ashes in his trademark drooped mustache. He had lost an eye in the woods when he worked on a holy day. But that is another story.

In the old days, George's father, Charlie, had made a living cutting down and peeling the slim black spruce trees to make canoe and bolt-hook poles for the log drivers. He also made axe, shovel, and rake handles. He was a master axe man who sometimes came home to our place at Keenan on the main river. He loved to have a drink with my father, share a few Cains River anecdotes, and then they would go fishing. On days like this, the men wore woolen red and black mackinaw coats and felt hats, the best possible woods clothing for wet, cold weather.

In his younger days, my uncle Alex had been first a country singer and then a go-preacher. As a boy, I sometimes travelled with him to different communities, setting up the tent, passing around the collection box, and on occasion playing the organ. But Alex gave up this life to become a log driver and river guide like my father and grandfather had been, although my father was also a successful storekeeper on the main river. Also, Daddy and Papa had staked a claim here on the Cains – not far from Buttermilk Brook – when a gold rush occurred in the early '50s. The claim was never worked so they lost it. But as far as I know there were never any minerals found on this river. These men had also canoed the Cains a hundred times, had tented or stayed in rustic river camps, fished salmon and trout, and hunted in the late autumn woods. There had always been something about this river that drew my family to its shores.

Maybe it was because my great-grandmother, Maggie Porter (of Irish descent), came from a place just a half-mile up the river from Buttermilk. A rock foundation, what remains of the old Andy Porter property, can still be found in a small clearing not far from where Salmon Brook makes its confluence with the Cains. This is a part of the family legacy of which I am proud, because two centuries later, there is still much folklore about the Porter family's life here. I have a portrait of Maggie Porter. It hangs on the wall in my cabin. It is in an oval frame with a convex smoky glass covering. In the photo she is a stern-faced, no-nonsense figure with pearl necklace and a large feather in her hat. Because that is the only likeness we have of her, she appears to me in that image when her name is mentioned here now.

George and I fished in the wind and rain all morning without a strike and the water started to come up because of the downpour. And I could hear wild geese, like dogs barking in the distance. Sometimes I got lost in meditation as I stared into the ancient water that dazzled me. Big salmon were jumping and rolling on their move upstream. I tried many of the fall-coloured fly-hooks – oranges, yellows, and reds – but had no luck. For a time I tried a number four orange-haired Ingles Butterfly and cast straight across the flow and stripped. But nothing worked.

"Andy, there's many big fish in here but they're not interested in anything I have in my fly box," George said, his voice rising and falling under the music of the water, his office face bronzed already from the wind and rain. He had waded in so deep he looked like the bust of Chopin.

"I could come back here after the water drops and the fish are taking," I told him. "But as in lovemaking, real or imagined, it is no fun catching fish when you are alone, although both these experiences give me the same thrill."

Having worn hip waders, I had been standing on a rock in centre stream and because of the rising river, I got soaked to the skin when I scrambled for footing in three feet of water and fell in, ass over tea kettle – the water fast as spit and as cold as December – in order to get to shore. Certainly, I had not inherited the strong river legs that run in my family. *Good Lord, show me the way.* I learned that in a river, it is easy to climb upon a rock on the upriver side where the water is more shallow, but almost impossible to get down from the same rock when the water is pushing against you. In truth, you have to get off the rock on the downriver side where the water is always deeper because of the back tow. This is tricky. Wet to the skin and cold, I took a belt of the Scotch whisky George had brought for medicinal purposes. We toasted one another and our former times here with the old folks, before going back to the grove to dry ourselves and have lunch. While it was a cold, blustery day, I was with real people and I found this to be a welcome contrast to Niagara's factory life where I had been working, in the heat and smog, without air conditioning, for over thirteen years since my divorce.

Our kinfolk were sitting by a hardwood fire, telling stories, while passing a bottle back and forth. And their whisky-enhanced laughter was ghostly. They were happier than I had ever seen them. And anyone who was canoeing past could have heard the hilarity and the singing, the coarse jokes and imaginings brought forth by the setting, the drinks, and a whole lot of nostalgia. They sang and told yarns with a childish simplicity, as if they were trying to make the trip live up to the illusions they had been nurturing about the adventure, a day they had been looking forward to for so long, and I suspect with internal visions of what it had been like in their youth. These were ancestral reflections, intertwined: the recounting of river adventures and the century-old habits of a not-so-elusive past.

For what else did they have to reflect upon but their own undying pleasantries? They would answer the call if necessary, do it all again. It was in their blood to cuff the logs, turn handsprings on the moving rafts, eat beans from tin plates in a river scow, sleep on the forest floor, and go home in the late spring with pockets filled with money. It reminded me of the fantasy lover, so imaginary, in a low-cut dress, that we carry in our minds, and which we try to make real; that person who is always available and true to us, the only one we will ever really possess in memory or in dreams.

Our appetites had been nourished by the damp autumn air, the water, and the whisky. It was here, in the rain, in the shelter of big trees, on a weathered board door, that I enjoyed a meal that was tastier than any I ever had in town. After a blessing by Uncle Alex – "Lord, thank 'e for the vittles. Amen." – we wolfed down the eggs and fried ham, the steaming biscuits and beans, the toasted, thick slices of homemade bread and cheese, the smoking black tea that was sweetened with molasses, a river camp dinner.

"You still have a real flavour in your voice," Cecil said to Uncle Alex. "You should get back into preaching."

"No goddamn way," he said. "I got me fill of that stuff when the local lads set fire to me tent and run me out of Howard back in '64. But I had a pretty good following for a while there, especially after I got on the radio broadcast. But I can see now that I had a false idea of how things would come down."

And then he said, "But I still got me old guitar. I s'pose I could go back to singin'."

And I was thinking that it was life itself and the booze that had borne away his young dreams and he turned to salmon guiding and river driving.

I was also thinking that a change in the weather, to a cold day of fog and rain, and a baptism were enough to create a fresh world within myself too, an incentive to move away from the unionized factory life and a desire to harmonize with the country, to escape the city's seclusion we are forced to live in as we grow older and are facing the winter exile. And I knew that I would not go back to Ontario; rather I would stay among my own people. Still, having mastered the city art of indifference and the keeping to oneself, I now felt a touch of melancholy and aloneness and I wished that the lover of my dreams could have been here beside me, but knew that she never would be. No man walks alone, by choice, I thought. And how I envied my father, who had the wisdom to hold on to a good woman, his million-dollar bride. For sure there was no melancholy in his veins.

Despite the ragged conversation, the local lingo which I had half forgotten, I was in no hurry to finish this outdoor meal. As the short fall day slipped past, I heard repeated stories from the same people about the same river – of the log-driving days, the brother-in-law who had gone under and drowned in the spring of '53, the canoe expeditions with the sports, and the times of hunting birds in those big pine tree summits along the banks of this river. All were enhanced by the drinks and the hyped-up recollections of tragedy that hit close to home, and of good times too with a funny twist of how uncle so-and-so had said a thing: the outside world being so far away, it was never in the picture.

At one time there had been plans for a railroad along the Cains and there was a sawmill at Sabbies, a tributary that supplied planks for the river's shipbuilders as well as commercial buildings and farms. My great-aunt Sarah's house in Keenan, which was built in 1843 from this planking, is still standing. And there had been a school where my aunt Lillian taught and lived in the apartment up over the classroom. There had also been plans for a church. But when in 1886 the new railroad took a more practical route and followed the Miramichi and Nashwaak rivers, from Newcastle to Fredericton, there was great disappointment among the settlers who were suffering hardship and death because of the river's remoteness. There was an exodus. "It doesn't take long to kill things," my father said. "Not like it does to make them grow."

Today there are abandoned farms, well grown over, from Wild Cat to Howard, the full length of this beautiful river. In these woods, you could stumble upon a crumbling rock cellar, a stone line-fence, or perhaps an open-shaft well. And I suspect that the siblings whose roots are in these places would have stories of their history. I know only of my own family's experiences in here.

This day, I stood by the fire until my clothes were dry, and even though it was still raining, we had those heavy-limbed spruce trees for shelter. From a distance, the scene would have resembled an antique photograph I had picked up at an auction sale. It was a depiction of a whaler's campfire: the glow of the fire, like a magic lantern, lighting the faces and trees that surrounded it, with darkness coming down. Or perhaps it was the sun's reflection that shines through the coloured chapel window in Howard.

As I listened to my father and Uncle Alex wax on about the Cains, this relative or that, this or that farm, it started to snow: big soft flakes that drifted up the choppy river to cling to the orange grass and the tree branches and turn the black shore boulders into polar bears. Winter was definitely in the air. In the short fall day, the approaching darkness was coming down fast, and we had to gather our things and head back up the hill, leaving our cosy campfire, the flameless embers smoking in the distance. It was not easy for George and me to get the old folks up that hill. Once we slid in the mud, back down halfway, and had to rely on the stunted growth trees and deep roots to give us a lift.

Sonny Ross

On a night in April Sonny Ross stole into Paula's bedroom. Sonny had come from Bradford a year before when his mother and father were killed in a car accident. He kept to himself and none of us had an ounce of trust in him. I heard the boards creak and thinking it was Hayward, reached under the pillow for a knife I had kept for my protection. Gripping its horn handle, I slipped out of bed, tiptoed across the hall, and eased the door open to peek in. In shirttails Sonny was watching Paula as she slept. The thought of what he was up to made me light-headed. I gasped for breath and my heart pulsated as I burst into the room.

Seeing the weapon, he pushed a chair in front of me just as Paula woke up. She did not scream but her eyes popped as I tried to get at Sonny. Then he jumped past me, knocking a picture from the wall as he streaked down the hall, not knowing how close he was to tasting that steel blade.

Paula screeched. Lights came on and Maria came running. She was followed by the other youths, some of whom were in a panic and crying. I explained that my surrogate sister was having a nightmare and I was trying to comfort her. Of course Maria did not believe this and when Paula held to the story, the maid scoffed and called her a slut. There was the usual confusion and then we all went back to bed. The incident was never mentioned by Sonny, Paula, or me. So it died like any bad dream that came out of a night's sleep. But it kept me awake for a few nights. I wondered if something was going on between Sonny and Paula. Plus the fact that I could not trust myself, especially when angered, and could have stabbed a surrogate brother frightened me. Every time I thought of it my head ached and I broke into a sweat. The only way I could measure my hatred was from the guilt I felt after I did something bad, and that was too late.

I knew I had to get along with lads like Sonny since they were part of our big so-called family. This was not easy as I was inclined to hold a grudge. More than once we snapped at one another at the supper table though no one else in the so-called family really understood why. Sometimes I got up and left before the meal ended.

"Try to get along, you two!" Maria shouted.

I found out early on that learning to *not* trust came easily whereas training myself to trust was next to impossible. For advice I counted on no one but Paula. And I knew that Sonny Ross had been sent to three foster houses and always came back to the Youth Home. So he was no angel either. But after the knife incident, there were times when I questioned Paula's reasoning. Had she invited him into her room? And why afterwards would she say nothing to put him down? "I must go to visit

Sonny," she would say. And I wondered if she sensed that I was jealous and would spy on her – jealous at not having found fidelity, despair at not being accepted.

One night I heard Paula crying, "I want Gram! Oh please God, bring back my Gram!"

I went across the hall and held her in my arms until she told me that all the bad feelings were gone. It is funny how a little hug can repair a soul from so much rejection.

"Oh, David, thank God you're here," she said. "I don't care what they say, you are a true brother."

When Paula heard me wheezing in the night or crying, which made my asthma worse, she came to my room. I did not want her to see me in that state and tried to hide it. I felt it took away from my manliness, an important thing when you're thirteen and trying to earn someone's love. But she always played it down, saying it was an allergy, that sensitive people suffered more because they felt more, and that it was really a virtue. "David, the same as for lonesome, the best cure for asthma is a good hug. It will chase away those fears that breed in the dark." She would pound me on the back as I inhaled the asthma relief, a summer savory-like herb Maria got for me from a specialist in Maine. I placed it in a saucer and set it sputtering with a lit match. I breathed through a swamp reed, coughed and spit into a chamber pot after blowing the smoke out my window so the smell would not upset Hayward, the head man.

I dreamed of having Paula, not as a sister or a nurse, but a lover. She had become my teenage fantasy. Some nights from out of a sound sleep she came to my bed through the door, but often the window, where a breeze made the curtain flap and the starlit river could be seen in reflection from the light of the big white moon. She was always dressed in a too-small nightgown and moving as silently as a ghost. I caressed her small breasts with the brown nipples, tasted her honey breath, so sweet and so beautiful. It was like we were eating the same hard candy, returning it to each other's mouths with a kiss. I hugged my pillow, feeling the moisture of her sex as I drifted into a lonely pleasure that ended in self-release, a hollow sense of well-being and a sound sleep.

Near the end of May in '56 Paula came down with whooping cough which quickly developed into pneumonia. Sonny got it first and was sent to the hospital. I knew something was wrong when Paula would not come to the shore for a smoke, knowing I had stolen a pack of Sweet Caporals down at the diner. She lay on a cot in the kitchen and shivered, even though it was a warm day. Her face was pale as candle wax but when I put a hand on her forehead it was on fire. When Maria took her to the doctor, Paula was raving about her grandmother being beside her. Paula was given a double dose of penicillin and taken to the hospital, where she slept down the hall from Sonny Ross. How had she caught Sonny's disease? What would stop him from going to her bed now? My torment was overpowering my love for her and making life miserable. I just wanted her back at the home, and well.

Paula had the bluest eyes I ever saw, eyes that sparkled when she got mad or even when she was being funny, which was seldom. But that night when I went to visit her in the hospital they were glazed and yellow.

"Paula, do what the nurses tell you and you'll be out of here soon!"

"I can't stand those big ugly nurses. And the food in here stinks!"

"But you have to ..."

"Jumpins, Dave, I'd give anything for a tailor-made cigarette," she said. "And bring me something to read."

The next day a nurse caught Paula smoking in the washroom. Of course I got the blame for taking in the tobacco. After that, nurses searched my pockets before letting me in to see her. When Paula told me she had made friends with a Mountie who dropped in to visit, I thought she was trying to upset me further. I laughed and told her the cop probably wanted her as an informer and nothing more. All the juvenile delinquents were considered to be thieves.

"But maybe he just likes me," she cried. "I can have a friend outside that stinking place, can't I?"

"You can have whoever you want!"

Paula was deeper than most and at times hard to figure out. She had become a reader, throwing herself into the best books from the library. And could she ever read. She would make the characters come to life and dance on the page, books I could not even understand, as she read aloud. She could also read people's eyes at a glance, spot a phony before they even spoke. By now too her taste in music had changed from Johnny Cash to Bob Dylan, a songwriter who had a worse voice, but a message she said that would be around a lot longer. When a Dylan song came on the radio, with its howls and harmonicas, she coaxed me to listen. Later she did the same with Joan Baez, a girl who Maria said had come from Mexico.

I visited Paula at the hospital every day and took flowers I picked from gardens along the street. But I did not have the face to call on Sonny. Nor did Paula go to see him, she said, because nurses told her that he was by then in an oxygen tent. I missed Paula like you wouldn't believe. I found it hard to steal cigarettes without her getting the attention of storekeepers, plus I was overtaken with the problems of everyday life with no one to share my miseries. When my asthma acted up, I suffered through it alone. Paula's understanding was always a comfort and I carried her inside me between hospital visits. These can be nice feelings when no one else in the world cares if you live or die.

I often woke up in the night with that emptiness, and I grieved for a mother and father I never really knew. I prayed to my own god to keep me together until I got a start, and I prayed to the Devil to step back and leave me alone, give me a chance. Maybe I was being guided in a sinful way, but I believed that every person, even a priest or a cop, given the right cause and if pushed hard enough, was capable of robbing, raping, or killing. And this included those who lived in the big houses downtown, though it was less likely to happen to them. They wanted for nothing and were not apt to condemn a system that worked in their favour. I believed that one person's enemy was another's hero, depending on the times and what was happening. But, unlike Paula's sickness, there were no injections to cure broken hearts or loneliness and no laws that could make these feelings go away.

"Wouldn't it be great if anger could be treated like pneumonia?" Paula said.

"Then I would come to the hospital with you, take the medicine."

To Paula, I took books I stole at the second-hand bookstore. But I wondered if Sonny was sneaking down the hall to be with her when I was not there. When I questioned her about this she said nothing. Paula was anything but a tattletale. (You learn that trait awfully young in a youth centre.) I thought about warning Sonny to keep away from her. But then, this night he came to me in a dream. We met face to face back on the ball field. He asked me to sit, as I did with Mum in a similar dream. He looked at me with tormented eyes.

"David, you know I would never hurt Paula. She is my sister too. My feelings for her are the same as for my blood sister who was taken from my family in Bradford when Daddy and Mummy died. I really miss little Anna, who is now living in East Falconer. But when I was lonesome in the night and tried to talk to Paula, you tried to kill me."

"Sonny, I'm so sorry!" I said, smelling his sweaty old jacket as I reached out to give him a hug. It is funny how we do all the right things in dreams; how we follow our hearts when we are sleeping and not when awake.

When I woke up, I felt a lot better about life and my new-found brother, a person who had gone through many of the same things as Paula and me. I decided to visit him at the hospital, set things straight.

But in the morning, when we finished breakfast, Maria and Hayward called all of us youths into the visiting room where the minister was sitting with some members of the committee. They asked us to stand in a circle and hold hands while the pastor told us we had to be strong, trust in the Lord, and that our brother Sonny was in Heaven because he had died the night before.

"There you go," Hayward said. "The Lord giveth and the Lord taketh away, like a thief in the night. We never know the hour, do we?"

Right away, Sonny Ross became the most loving brother anyone could have. And I felt I was the worst person in the world for not seeing it before. I became lightheaded, and the room started to spin. I had to run outside so I would not throw up on the floor. I was trying to cry but I could not make it happen. I vomited tears. I went to my room and got into bed in hopes that I could bring back the dream. Then I walked to the hospital where the nurses had not broken the news to Paula. As I talked to her, I felt a surge of selfishness and wanted to share Sonny's love with her. But I kept it all inside. I kept it all inside and grieved for Sonny Ross. And I cried for the fate of Paula, who would not take orders from the nurses. What would happen to me if I lost her?

"Dave, what's eating at you today?" she said. "Your eyes are filled with pain."

"I'm okay, sister, I'm okay."

Paula was not told of Sonny's death until some days later when she felt better. And her knowing it somehow made me feel relieved because she understood, having seen us fighting, what I had been going through. At least I had someone to share my feelings with.

In the afternoon Maria asked the youths to gather wildflowers and then to write a letter to our brother. In silence we walked the hillside and riverbank. We picked daisies, dandelions, buttercups, and violets as well as fifteen yellow tulips I was able to steal off the lawn down at the post office. We stood these in pickle jars, pop bottles, milk containers, and soup cans. They made a sweet smell in the shabby old front room. We attached our notes of love and forgiveness to the blossoms.

In the evening we were dressed in our best T-shirts and blue jeans when the undertakers, in their black suits and gray-striped neckties, came from Kent's Funeral Home and wheeled Sonny's cloth casket in the front door and opened it for viewing. Again I was sick and started shaking. It was a long time before I could get up the nerve to go in where the remains were. I thought, if only Paula could be here to hold my hand.

For the next two days Sonny Ross lay among that cluster of wilting wildflowers. Dressed in a white sports coat, shirt, and black tie the minster had bought, his hands were clean, his hair combed over one eye. His mustache had just started to sprout and so was never shaved. We shook hands with people we did not know or want to know – folks from town, the school district, and the House Committee. Sonny's school class came in a group and praised our brother for all the qualities he never had. Some of Sonny's blood relations from Bradford visited, but I never saw his sister Anna and wondered if she was just a spirit from the dream. Real or abstract, she would always be a ghost now.

Through this, Maria walked about, holding her prayer beads, dabbing her eyes. She had become a woman of extremes, laughing one minute and crying the next.

Hayward was stern and red-cheeked from booze, his eyes empty and dry. Near the front door he set up a small table where, like a timekeeper, he took orders for Gideon Bibles.

I did not stand in the receiving line because until the night he died, everyone in the house knew I had no use for Sonny Ross. I didn't want to look like a total hypocrite. But while his remains were in the house I was not able to close an eye. I could not eat, yet I was not hungry. Through those long nights, I tossed and turned and my asthma acted up. I smoked the herbs and blew the smoke out my window. Of course there was no sympathy for me. Sonny had become a hero to all the youths, many of whom sat up all night with the remains. It was a way to express their love for him and to deal with other things that were missing in their lives. As if this would relieve them from all hurts that would follow. Or the ones they already suffered.

Nor could I go into the wake room when visiting hours were over. It was as if I did not want to face my brother, even now in death, especially in death. I wanted to remember him with the sparkle in his eyes, even as we fought. I wanted to remember him as always being young, the person I had known young. Wishing Paula were near to help me deal with this, and fearing she might come to the same fate, I dressed, slipped out the kitchen door, and went back to the hospital, hoping to get a hug, but the place was locked, a night-watchman at the door.

On the third day all of us gathered in the parlour

and the minister read the prayers. Maria in her flowered housedress, without makeup or beads, sang Sonny's favourite hymn, "Yes, Jesus Loves Me." Then six of my brothers and two sisters carried the casket out the front door and into the back of a black station wagon. We walked behind the hearse down Albert Street, which was shaded by a canopy of trees, to St. Paul's Cemetery. The smaller ones carried the flowers. I could feel the other orphans' grief as we walked, holding hands like we had bonded against the hereafter. Robins and blackbirds chirped in the trees and there was the smell of lilac on the wind.

In the graveyard we stood with Sonny's hymn being sung, off-key, inside us and we listened for one good reason why we should believe in the everlasting soul. We pretended to hear and to understand yet another preacher trying to comfort us. While our brother was lowered into the ground and fresh clay shovelled over the coffin with a hollow sound, and daisies and buttercups scattered over the mound of newly turned earth, a freight train laboured past, sounding its lonesome whistle that echoed along the river, and leaving a strong smell of burnt diesel fuel about the town.

Then we all wandered off in silence, each trying to find comfort in his or her way.

For the next nine days, we wore black socks and black bands of crepe paper pinned to a sleeve. This period of mourning, Maria said, was an old Mexican tradition. I did not do it because I felt it would be wrong. Everyone knew Sonny and I were not friends, though I felt a great sorrow for how I treated him. I prayed that he would come back to me in a dream so we could talk again.

On the tenth day Paula stole out of the hospital. During visiting hours, in her bare feet and smock, she walked out the front door, hid in the trees along the street, and made her way back to the Home. She sneaked up the stairs and hid in the closet where she appeared like a ghost to frighten me. Her eyes were uneasy, her skin white as chalk. She whispered for me to give her a cigarette. Then she went to her room. And I thought that she was a child who never had the chance to be young.

In the evening, the hospital called looking for Paula. And two Mounties came to question Maria, who did not even know she was upstairs. They questioned me too. But I told them I had not seen her. A letter was sent over to the Youth Home, signed by the hospital board and doctors, claiming they were no longer responsible for Paula McKenzie. But she was better by then anyway. It was great to have her home.

Lost

The old homestead – the gray, weather-beaten farmhouse with the stained-glass windows encircling the front door; the upstairs dormers; the long, spooled veranda that faced the road; the worm-eaten shutters; and the chimney that was now strangled with ivy – was a welcome sight. Labouring under the weight of my duffle bag, plus the emotional burden of what I had been through in France, I walked down the road toward the front gate. I was choking to hold back tears. Along the gravel highway in front of the house, the ancient pine trees sighed and tossed their limbs in a kind of welcome. And there was a rattling of cattails in the umber pond where I had once kept a few ducks. I stood in the yard and looked at the old black barns that needed repair after the three long years I had been away: the mossy thatch of the cowshed, the rusted Ferguson 35 tractor, the '41 Ford pickup, the plank wagon box I had bought at the sawmill in Lockstead. And old times – the innocent little experiences I had as a boy, the brief adult times I had shared with my wife and son – came back to me. I shivered with emotion.

I slipped through the back door into the big kitchen, with its long-arm water pump that squealed when you pulled down on the handle and the wood-burning range, still warm, around which was the social centre of the household, down the hall and upstairs to my bedroom. The familiar old home smells and sounds were still here. It was the scent of bulk tea, burnt beans, cigarette ash, smoke from the stove, and a breeze in the ivy that clung to the veranda screening. They brought back a series of memories: the card games, hunting in the autumn wood, the Sunday aroma of a deer roast in the oven.

I wondered why Edna and Darren were not at home to greet me. (Perhaps they had not gotten my letter.) I changed into civilian clothes – it was great to be in civvies again – hung my uniform in a safe place in the big attic over the kitchen, whose windows gave onto the river, and wandered down the stairs and out into the yard. A tang of autumn was in the breeze and from a distant field a bird sang tenderly on one note. But there were no hens in the coop and the cow was gone from the stable. And there was no sign of Jasper, my old Jack Sullivan terrier. I wondered if my family, through a hard winter, had sold or butchered the cow. I knew this had often been done by families in times of hardship.

I remembered the April night of my marriage to Edna. At the wedding reception, we had drunk tea at this farmhouse. The women gathered in the kitchen to talk, and the men got together in the front room – it had a ghost of Edna's mother, Sadie, who had been waked there, five years before – to play cards. Secretly, I drank some rum and was in heaven. Boyd Williams, one of the men at the card table, so old and shaky that he stuttered and repeated himself when he talked, looked like one of those people we see carved on the doors of tombs or on plaques in churchyards – for sure a living gravestone, but with the temerity of a Texan. He was killed by a bolt of lightning later that summer in that same room, when he came into the house out of a storm and sat down on a chair with his back to an electrical plug-in outlet. The lightning came in on the wires and killed him instantly. And this brought another ghost to haunt the old living room. But my uncle Willie, the kindest and most religious man in Grand Rapids, said that Boyd was not a man to fear, dead or alive, not any more than Sadie had been, and that they were "the nicest little souls in the dear wide world."

I went back into the house, sat in the old bare living room, and looked about the place that was filled with things I remembered from before I went away. Everything here spoke to me and was linked to some feeling. But after being in posh places in England and France, the house looked small and shabby. The old cot, the parlour stove, the pump organ with its covered keyboard were still in their places. The chair where Boyd had been killed was replaced with a lamp table. And there was the homespun country painting, my mother's handiwork – I had brought it down from Howard after the wedding – that featured a grouping of honeysuckle and wild shore roses, daisies, and buttercups, with a drone of bees in the air. This artwork always inspired the beautiful images of that old world of my youth, things that were somewhere between life and schoolbooks. I could still see my mother's homely figure on the pathway from the barn as she carried two pails of warm milk in a shoulder yoke. I thought, art is long and life is short. The image still reminded me of a story entitled "All in A Day's Work" from my grade six reader.

Back then, each fall when the leaves were red and yellow, the high clouds made black moving patches on the mountain slopes, the wind had swung to the northwest, and a nip of frost was in the air, after school with my slingshot I took a walk to look for grouse. (I have always found a kind of contentment in the woods and fields, especially in those lonely hours, the long shadows of Indian summer.) On my way to the headwaters of McKenzie Brook, I walked the old truck roads. How long they were, yet with my young legs, how fast the farm was left behind. I stole through the tall yellow grasses of the beaver meadows from whence the brook flows, hearing the chuckle of the water below the dam, listening for the partridge's danger signals, getting a glimpse of that game bird that always flew away before I got near it. It had been the chase that mattered, boy after game that was never game. Those simple little things appear like a dream to me now, and I miss that old day of innocence, the melancholy recollections of past grandeur. I have come to realize that the best paradise is from my youth, the paradise I have lost. Back then I had never saved a dime, as dreamers never do. It had all been about living in the moment, the creative mind.

Knocking ashes from my cold pipe, I filled it with tobacco I had stolen from a high-end smoke shop in Paris and struck a match. Breathing in deep, the flavour tingled my insides and filled the room with a blue haze. And I thought what a marvelous thing good tobacco is, so filled with magic. For a brief moment the pleasures I got out of the flavour took me on a journey inside myself. Heigh-ho! I could see my loved ones, old and new, beckoning to be hugged, Edna on fire in my arms, my son in a Mounted Police uniform. I could see the best of a harvest coming from fields that had gone fallow, a successful fishing season, even though the water was high after the rains, a good deer hunt, sheds filled with hardwood for the kitchen and parlour stoves. By and by my pipe burnt out and my thoughts drifted back to normality.

I could clearly remember those last weeks at home and how I had been terrified to leave Edna and Darren – my son was then four years old – to look after the farm. I had been afraid to leave them and also fearful to go to war. But I had read an editorial in *The Standard* that stated, "If a young man is not at the front it is because he is afraid." So I enlisted, thinking that my flat feet and my faked asthma would keep me out of the army. However, against my wishes I was accepted. I had been so scared that I shivered in my boots. But Edna and Darren never noticed this fear in me as I joked and covered it by saying, "Don't grieve, you lads, I'll be back in a month or so." It seemed like I had to go overseas to prove to myself and to the river community that I was not a coward like so many men, not of the voluntary class, who hid in hollow logs when the army came looking for recruits. There were many who deserted after they had been recruited and passed the medical exam. Some were turned down because they were thought to be queer, and this became an act for people who were afraid.

Until, under a black sky, I hugged my small family at the station in Falconer, got on the train, took my seat, and waved goodbye from the coach windows. The train pulled away slowly and they were left standing on the plank siding, getting smaller and smaller as the distance between us grew and they were out of sight, physically. It was not only my family that I grew away from that day; it was a way of life, a circumstance shelved forever, to be recounted in the after-years of the conflict. On a radio, the song played, "We'll meet again, don't know where, don't know when, but I know we'll meet again some sunny day." I cried openly. It was okay to cry, now that I was away from family. There would be no shame in tears under the circumstances. I think that in retrospect, leaving my home and young family had been in some ways worse than the war itself.

After the train ride to Montreal and then back to Halifax, sitting among recruits of the North Shore Regiment, 3rd Canadian Infantry Division, men who were also pretending not to be afraid, I boarded a ship destined for Portsmouth, England, where the troops were so busy with training and strategy sessions on how to defeat the Germans, there was not much time to think. Later, in France, I had many comrades to share my feelings with, people who were terrified and expressed it openly because, according to the commissioned officers, men fought better when they were afraid, and hungry. These things bonded us into a large international family. And we loved one another. Yet, in spite of these people around me, I found the army to be the loneliest place on Earth. Still, I now miss those men, many of whom never made it back home. For sure the battle field was no place for a sentimentalist.

One in particular, a youth from Quarryville – he had

lied about his age to get into the army when his girlfriend left him – who had been shot in the chest and legs by a sniper, lay in the combat zone in such pain that he was delirious. In and out of consciousness, he raved about being home. I held him in my arms and comforted him. And the boy called me "Daddy."

"Daddy, I'm home now finally," he said. "We have things to do together."

"Yes, you are home now, son. But please try to get some rest."

I held the boy in my arms as he drifted into the big sleep. Later his body was tossed onto a stretcher to be carted away for burial. There had been prayers by the chaplain Raymond Hickey, who was a big part of the troop and had been reported missing in action for a time himself. (Later, Major Hickey would be awarded the Military Cross for bravery.) There would be a letter, edged in black, going to the boy's mother and father in Canada. I had sent a note to the family, saying that I had been with their son when he died, and that he had not suffered.

And there were two young men from Bathurst who had been killed in a fire fight with a German platoon. They had died together in a cornfield, both having been shot in the back. I had also written to their parents, saying they had not suffered and that they were buried in France.

There had been a lot of shooting this day. The enemy fire was coming from the basement of a pink cement house. One bullet struck the stock of my rifle, splintering it into shreds and numbing my right hand. It was then I pulled the cap off a hand grenade and tossed it in through the cellar's open window. There was screaming, a great bang, and a puff of smoke. Moving closer, I peeked in through the window to see a civilian woman and two small boys lying dead on the earth floor. And right away I realized that I did not have the common sense to be a good soldier. I just wanted to go home, back to Grand Rapids, New Brunswick, before I took another innocent life. There were times when I wondered if this actually happened or if it had been a nightmare I lived through every time I was under fire.

For me, these were experiences that could not be wiped away by a train ride back to the old home place, a "welcome home" party down at the Legion Hall, or a ceremony on Remembrance Day at the cenotaph. They were moments that came to me in the night and brought me out of a sound sleep. And I woke up screaming, while first looking for someone to shoot and then someone to hug.

I thought, I, like Ishmael in *Moby Dick*, am left to tell the tale. But of course I knew I would never talk about those things around home. In war, the soul of a man is stripped naked, his courage, or lack thereof, exposed for the world to see. There are no words to accurately describe the horror scenes I carry inside, and for comfort and peace of mind, I return, if only metaphorically, to the days of my boyhood, the open valleys down by the river where I used to ramble, the spruce grove on the hilltop where I had built a camp, the partridge hunting along McKenzie Brook.

I sat in the homemade rocking chair in the old living room and tried to put the pieces of my now scattered existence back together. Broken was my body and broken too my spirit. I knew these things would take some time to heal from, if ever. The house was cold and I started a fire in the glass-fronted stove. The smell of a wood fire was a comfort to me. I had grown up in a world of plow horses, old plank barns with the gray hue that time had given them, threshing machines, and salmon nets, ten miles up the river, and moved down here to Grand Rapids after the wedding. I had been naive before I went away, sheltered but happy in this community where I worked in the woods, gardened, fished the fathomless waters of Southwest Miramichi, guided the foreign anglers, and poached moose and deer to keep the family eating. There had been card parties and once in a while a dance in the village where, after dressing in our best work clothes, me and my buddies went to dance with the stout, rural-faced women and where overweight, cigarette-smoking men scuffed around to the screeching of cheap fiddles.

Once at a dance in Falconer, someone who lived in a shack on Maple Ridge had beaten the bejesus out of me because I flirted with his girlfriend. For a time, there was a feud between the families, emotions that were brought back years later by the cries of a violin. But, just the same, it had been a good place to grow up, with all the community, all the social life that anyone would need. I was going over these things in my mind when I heard talking and looked out to see Edna and a youngster – it would be Darren – coming in the lane. Each was carrying a basket of apples. They had obviously been down to the long-abandoned Campbell place where we used to go in the fall to gather wild crabs for stewing. I ran up the stairs where I waited for them to come into the house. And the sound of Edna and Darren's voices in the kitchen brought back a strong sense of love, happiness, and home.

After some time, hearing the squeal of the pump, I stole down the steps and into the kitchen. I walked up behind Edna, who was washing apples in the sink. Putting my arms around her, I squeezed. I held her in this position for a few seconds, until I got a sharp elbow in the ribs. It was then she swung around and we embraced long and hard. "Oh, Randy," she said and rubbed my back while still in the kiss. "Oh, Randy, you're home. You're home finally."

Darren, who had been in the dining room, came out with a rifle pointing at me.

"You get out of our house!"

"It's okay, Darren, put the gun away. It's your father."

Darren put down the gun, came over, and hugged us both. It was a group hug that lasted for a long time. Finally, I let them go and went over and sat in the rocking chair. Convulsing, I tried to hide my tears. We were all blabbering and wiping our eyes. "It's an emotional old time for us all," I said.

"There is no disgrace in tears," Edna told us. "But there is disgrace in having no feelings at all."

In the yellow lamplight of the supper table, we ate roast beef and potatoes, with stewed apples and rhubarb for dessert.

"This is the best meal I've had in years. I missed your good cooking."

"You likely ate better in England and France," Edna said. "I'm just a farmhouse cook, is all I am."

"I grew up eating farmhouse cooking. The tastes are filled with happy times."

And so it was, in the few short days it took to reacquaint with my family, to eat together and sleep together, to pray together and lay together, to meet the neighbours and get caught up on the news, who had died and who had had babies, to slip back into the old home smells, the homely barn-scented work clothes, the fragrance of the wood fires that always brought my mother, long deceased, to my side. The sour manure heap from the near barn carried the ghost of my father: following the horses and plow across the river intervale, and then sitting on the binder as it crossed the yellow oat fields.

I enjoyed the scent of the winter's stove wood, the sawdust smells after its cutting; maple and birch blocks that had to be put into the shed. And there were wind brakes to be put up on the north side of the yard, with Darren helping after school. There had been the regular trips to Charlie Bowman's store for groceries and gossip.

In doing these things, though emotional, I slowly became just another river man, a woodsman and farmer who fished for salmon, hunted for deer, and worked seasonally in the lumber woods for the Grand Rapid Lumber Company. And in the evenings, by my bed lamp, from my old school readers, the only books in the house, I read the adventurous stories of Harwood Steel, William Henry Drummond, Gladys Francis Lewis, and the Mohawk Princess E. Pauline Johnson. And the escape, back to my boyhood, so intimate with nature – the grassy school grounds, the rural churchyard, mission bells that appealed to my young ears – helped me to forget the war and sleep well. I found that, like a bird song or a train whistle, the scenes in my readers brought back the emotions I had experienced when I read them originally, a state of mind otherwise inaccessible.

Edna and Darren, with the help of a neighbour, had indeed butchered the cow, sold the hide, and salted the meat. And the old dog had died. They had raised potatoes enough for the winter. And from Darren's cucumber patch, they made pickles and were now in the process of stewing apples. I put a net in the river and caught enough salmon to fill a salt barrel. But we also needed deer meat, and one morning when there was the threat of snow in the wind, I took my old 30-30 carbine, a sleeping bag, and some camping supplies and went to the headwaters of McKenzie Brook to look for a deer.

It was a long walk on paths that had grown over from lack of use. But I knew the lay of the land and where the lonely brook with its moss-covered rocks, a place where I had angled for trout before going away, was headed. I had grown up in the woods, knew the habits of the animals, and after being overseas, I just could not get enough of those spruce groves and stunted juniper barrens, the talking brook, a glad song in my ears. It became a place to heal, the trees being friends that talked back to me when the wind blew, especially the king of the forest, those whispering pines, so high above the others, scattered upon the landscape.

I had been gone for three days, slept by a campfire on those late autumn nights, warmed beans on flameless coals, and ate out of the frying pan. I was looking for a deer, yes, but also to be at one with nature. *I am never alone in a grove of trees*, I thought. *They are trusted living things.* On those dark November days, after the preliminary cold snap, there was no heat from the sun. I trod in the frozen swamps – the river was frozen over also – and for food I set rabbit snares up on the ridges, picking my way on a cushion of dead leaves through a maple and beech wood, crunching along, viewing the big stands of leafless timber, while looking for the horizontal curves that would be a deer. At this time of year, these animals were gray and motionless. Like ghosts, they would stand and watch you, especially the bucks that were looking for does, for it was the rutting season.

On the fourth day, I knew a big storm was pending because there had been a hazy sundog that morning. I knew too that I had better get back to the farmhouse to be with Edna and Darren through the impending bad weather. The more I thought about this the more serious it seemed. I half-ran toward the river which, according to my compass – it was held away from the gun that made its directional arrow twirl like a chip in an eddy – was due east. At such times only a compass can tell you where you really are. Of course this did not allow for the big bend in the watercourse just downstream from the house. Snowflakes began to filter down through a lattice of gray limbs – they had green clumps of clinging moss – picking up with the wind until it was hard for me to see.

I wanted to get as far out as possible before the early winter darkness overtook me, because all I had for a light was a small oil lantern that was by then low in fluid. I followed the compass's directional arrow, which appeared to be taking me deeper into the woods, until, frustrated, I threw the gadget into the trees and decided to follow my own instincts. I had never been a compass man anyway and always relied on my own awareness, like an artist does to academics.

I knew the landmark trees that would lead me to the house and into the summer kitchen where a fire would be burning in the old Star stove, a range that had two ovens, because due to the storm, my family would be expecting me tonight. This was where, if I was lucky, I would hang my deer from a hand-hewn beam and proceed to butcher it with Edna and Darren giving a hand. But I could not find my way out of the woods. And twice I came upon my own tracks in the new snow, which meant I had been travelling in circles. Again McKenzie Brook was chuckling just under the hill. The snowflakes were striking my face and melting. And there was sleet, like broken razor blades that bounced off my mackinaw coat. The trees cracked and snapped like rifle fire. And this gave me the impressions that I was being shot at, or perhaps being buried alive. Suddenly, I was fearful of the wilderness, afraid that my own sanctuary would swallow me up. And for a time, I felt that the big city, with all its opportunities for renewal and growth, was where I needed to be.

Overheated under the wool clothing, I was in this confused state of mind when I saw a deer standing ahead of me on the trail. It was a good-sized buck, enough meat to feed my family for the winter. I raised the gun and took aim. *Boom! Boom!* The shots were short and fast, like the one-two punches of a skilled boxer. And there was no echo. The deer disappeared and I figured I had killed it. But when I went to where my prey had been standing, there was no sign of an animal, not even a track on the empty, snow-covered trail.

I pondered this for a while and felt I might have been imagining things. I laughed at myself, a mocking, hearty laugh that was muffled by the trees, the snow, and the frosty winds. I must not tell this to anyone, I thought. Actually, I was glad there had not been a deer because I had no idea where in the woods I was and how I would get an animal home. It was more important for me to get out of the woods, back to my family. But what direction would I go on an evening that was growing darker by the minute?

There was only the snapping of branches, the whisper of winds that seemed to smother me in an endless waste of snow. I stood in a small clearing and shouted at the top of my voice. Then I fired my rifle into the air, three times, an old distress signal. But the sounds of the gun appeared to be muffled by the blizzard. I hollered to the distant trees, "Please, oh please, please, please, you are my friends. Help me out of this mess. Help me find my way! Help me find myself!"

I decided that I would have to head back to the grove of spruce – how far it was on my half-drifted-over backtracks – build a shelter out of boughs, start a fire, and stay in this cover until morning, hoping all the while that the storm would blow through overnight. In the morning, I would melt some snow for tea, fry up some rabbit meat, head east toward the sunrise, the big river. I knew I had to keep my head straight as I had heard stories about people who were lost having been overtaken by panic and that they walked in circles and raved because the woods were closing in on them. This thought brought hot waves of blood that surged through my brain, leaving me dizzy. I had also heard stories about people being found in the woods after being lost for days or weeks and they were always on their knees, crawling like a bear, in their desperate attempts to find their way. I must not let that happen to me, I thought. I must keep a cool head.

For a brief moment, in reflection, I was back on the battlefield, hiding behind a rock while looking for the ghosts that could bring me down. It was like I was running from the things I feared, more so than one who was looking for the things I loved. Since the war I had always been conscious of illusions, the shadowy figures that could sneak up behind me and put a bullet in my back. And I believe it was a state of delirium and guilt from my impulsive actions in France that had killed innocent people. This I lived through many times. And there was more.

Campbell and Leonard. I must ask their forgiveness for not giving them more support when they were under fire. At the Officers' Mess, during their Friday night pool game, would these men be laughing at my cowardly conduct? Would they show any hospitality toward a witty man? Maybe they are also dead because of me. I tried to put these men out of my mind, but they kept popping up through the night. I thought, it is fodder for a story for sure, but a tale that I don't have the words to accurately describe. It is not easy for a man to write about his own wit, his cowardly ways. It is just too painful and a thing that has to be worked through. Maybe down the road, I will be able to do it justice, through forgetfulness of others and my own imagination, which has a way of softening a troubled past so that everything from that day becomes a dream. And the writing of it into fiction will put it out of my mind, put it on a shelf, once and for all.

Sitting beside my dancing flame, I lit my pipe. The tobacco smoke mixed with the wood smoke to smell like home. I said to the fire, "You are my friend tonight. We are in this together." I put my back to a big pine tree, covered myself with the sleeping bag and some fir boughs, and tried to doze off. I felt that a good night's rest would help clear my head. But when I closed my eyes, I could see, in the distance, Edna and Darren beckoning to me. I threw the covers aside, got up, and walked in their direction. Bent double against the wind, and gasping for breath, I tried to approach them. But when I got near, they retreated, only to beckon again before fading into nothingness. "There it is, that goddamned old ghost!"

I knew that back at the house, Edna and Darren would be walking the floor from window to window. They would have left the outside lights turned on so that if I came to the field's edge, however desperate, I would be able to find my way to the house. Of course they knew if I made it that near to home I would not need a light, as the earthworm glow from windows would be casting their rectangular patterns on the snowy dooryard. They would feel helpless as they waited through the night, while the bitter winds moaned around storm doors and loose upstairs windowpanes. For them it would be a night of pacing the floor and praying, a time when neither of them would close an eye.

I sat through the long night, wrapped in the sleeping bag, under a roof of birchbark and fir boughs. My moistened clothing grew stiff and froze into a plastic-like covering. But I was not cold. I was in Paris, on leave, on a breezy summer night I had spent there with three of my comrades, in our summer uniforms, walking along the Champs-Élysées, viewing the fashions of the young women and men who came and went from the big restaurants and theatres. One of those women, a barmaid, flirted with me. She had sat on my knees on a street-side bench, threw her arms around my neck, and kissed me on the cheeks. For ten dollars she slept with me that night in the Victor Hugo Hotel. Young as she was, she appeared to be a deep thinker, though troubled within. And I was sorry I had let the sex happen. Now, I wished I was back there and with that classic woman in my arms. But then I wondered if she was real, or had she also been born of a dream? Real or imagined, she had left an image of kindness with me, the gentleness and class of Paris, France.

Months later, on a fall night in Paris, I walked into a high-class clothing store. It was very busy as people were buying clothing for the yuletide recitals. A salesman asked if I needed assistance. I told him that I was fine and being looked after by another clerk. In the changing room, I put on a pinstripe brown suit, overcoat, and gray felt hat. Then I walked out the door and down the street. And to this day I wonder if my crime had ever been discovered.

Briefly now, I can see the smile in the blue depths of my mother's eyes when her day's work was done, the skim milk separated from the cream. Her silence spoke louder than words. I knew that I must not disappoint her, because she had put a lot of faith in me and my being successful in life. "Randy has class," she used to say. She would never know of my fatal mistakes overseas. She did not need to know this about her favourite son. For a brief moment now, to escape, I was in the Old West of my school readers, with stories such as "Across the Ribbon of Steel." Those innocent sketches, all so well described by Susanna Moodie and Catherine Parr Traill, stayed in the mind's eye through life: the elevator towns along the CPR, the stampeding wild horses, the buffalo hunts, the Mounted Police. These, and the farm stories of Sinclair Ross, provided special places in the mind that my boyhood knew so well. These locations I still escape to in times of trouble.

Indeed, I had been a dreamer in my boyhood. But they had been dreams that reached no farther than my father's line-fences, those short-range images of my youth: the imaginative powers that carried in their descriptions the simple country ways, the one-room school, the little church to which my family had donated a stained-glass window, the old religious superstitions, and my fear of the divinities. After some minutes, my mind turned to my wife and son, perhaps wandering about the woods looking for me, or back on the river in our comfortable old farmhouse. I knew that was where I really wanted to be, if I was lucky enough to survive this night and make it home. I thought, I must learn to think deep; that old day of dreaming about what would never be is gone. Those coarsened and crayoned boyhood days, the remembrances and their pleasant little imaginings, within reach back then, have long since grown over and can only be retrieved through the pages of an elementary schoolbook. And the chase has now ended for me too, I can see that now. There would be no sport in hunting down an animal that I would not kill. I am not here for destruction. I am here for the mending.

When daylight finally started to break through the trees, now laden with snow, I could see that the storm was over, the wind having died, the eastern sky coppered, the blood red sun, twice its normal size, as if to make a point, peeking over the horizon. In a tree over my head, a chickadee chirped, *"Don't give it up. Don't give it up,"* and there was the *"peep"* of a moose bird that came to sit on my arm and brighten the lonesome campsite. I stoked my fire and cooked some rabbit meat before heading out in a direction toward the sunrise, due east, which should take me out to the big river. The walking was hard in the knee-deep snow and I figured I was still in the headwaters of McKenzie Brook because I could still hear the water chuckling in my head. But as I travelled, I noticed that the countryside was dropping off in a long downhill slope. Then I came upon some old familiar landmarks, the red dogwood-fringed intervale, the line-fence, the pasture gate, and I knew that I had spent the night within an arrow's flight of my now sleeping winter fields.

Angels of Mercy

A t my apartment after a long day at the mill, I threw off my work clothes, got into the shower, scrubbed under my nails, and rinsed my hair until it squeaked. With a towel around me, I poured a tall glass of scotch and drank it straight down. It was hot in the apartment, the air stale, and all I could think about was how I was going to cool off, get the mill mentality out of my head. The Maritime Paper Makers Union was like an orphanage in that there were so many fools who would have you follow their lead. I sat a while and smoked. Then I put on a light shirt, shorts, and sandals, went out, got into my car, and drove around Bradford. The sidewalks were filled with young people. I parked and went into the Radio Café where I sat at the bar and listened to Wade Weaver, a singer from upriver.

Some young women in a booth at the back were noisy. Wade said the one who had green eyes and barley-coloured hair was Wilma Johansson. When I looked at her, she held my gaze and smiled. Wilma was slim, in a red blouse, khaki shorts, and sandals, her legs white as flour. Her smile picked me up, so I went over and introduced myself. She did not speak; instead she giggled and looked at the floor. Then all of them got up and hurried outside. I finished my drink, went out, and stood against the building to watch the traffic flow by. The hot breeze pushed around the rock 'n' roll music as engines revved and tires squealed. I tramped my cigarette into the sidewalk. Maybe I would check out the Nurses' Residence.

Approaching my car, I was surprised to see Wilma sitting on the right front fender. She had one knee up and the other leg stretched out on the hood, like a photo I had seen of Marilyn Monroe. Her demeanour held both a threat and a promise. She jumped in beside me and her hair whispered. I could smell her shampoo as she helped herself to a cigarette from my shirt pocket. And I thought, help yourself there, Wilma.

She said, "Give me a light, bad boy."

As I held a lit match, she puffed and coughed, so I knew she was not really a smoker.

Wilma told me that she lived in Smith Falls and was employed at Zellers. When I started the engine, she moved in close and rested an arm on my shoulder. I thought, nothing takes the anger out of a man's soul like a good woman. My heartbeat quickened when she turned up the radio's volume in the way that Paula, my old girlfriend from the Home, used to do. With the hair and dimpled smile, she was from out of a dream. She wiped away all bitterness from the conversations down at the mill. I felt a surge of ego: it was so nice to drive with a woman beside me in the old convertible, if only for show. I drove past Paula's place, twice, hoping she would see us, but there was no one on her apartment's balcony. The radio played "I Got You

Babe" as we cruised down George Street and up the King's Highway and Wilma's hair blew straight back. Then I cut across to Albert Street, pulled into the driveway, and we went into the apartment.

We sat on the carpet and drank beer. I pulled her close and we kissed, the way people do who are intoxicated. Or just do not give a damn. Well, I guess we were intoxicated, and did not give a damn. The screen door was fastened, a breeze blowing the scent of blossom and river into the room. As I put flesh and blood to an old fantasy, I measured each move against the illusion. For a brief moment she was Paula. And I wondered if every woman I got involved with would be measured in that way. But she was Paula's size and demeanour all around.

Afterwards, we sat on the sofa and smoked, her blond legs folded under her. And her hair hung down like hay-thatch on a shed. I thought, it all happened too easily. Right away, I realized I did not know this young woman and felt an impulse to take her home. But she seemed in no hurry to leave. So I lit a candle, put a record on the hi-fi – some guitar music by The Ventures.

But when I turned around, she was wiping her eyes.

"Oh, that's Tony's favourite tune," she sobbed.

"Tony? Who the fuck is Tony?"

"He looks so much like you. We broke up last week. I miss him so much and ..."

"Oh, sweet Jesus!"

I turned off the record player and drove her home.

In the night, I woke up in a sweat. I was wondering how old Wilma was. We had not talked about age. We had not talked about anything. We had assaulted one another's ghosts.

On a morning in August, I got up early, put on my best golf shirt and slacks, and headed to the golf course. I would play eighteen holes and be back by midday. As I drove the River Road, there was no traffic, but the breeze was already burning my face and arms. I turned on the radio and then I turned it off, the better sounds coming from the birds in the big trees. I was thinking of how I would play the fairways and the concentration needed to make the putts. The night had left no dew, so the greens would be the same speed all morning.

As I neared the club, sounds of a motor-scooter brought me out of my game. I glanced into the rear-view mirror to see a biker following close. I could almost hear the metallic sounds of the Beach Boys song, *"First gear, it's allllright, second gear, it's allllright, faasssterrrrr."* The bike wavered as it was fed gas in spurts, so that it bleated out and then fell silent to coast. A blond-haired woman was driving and the wind made her white blouse puff out like a sail. She honked the tinny horn and waved. I pulled over and she drove up behind me on the clipped boulevard and kicked a lever so the scooter would stand alone. Dismounting, she lifted her sunglasses and stretched toward a handlebar mirror to adjust her hair. It was Wilma, a woman I had not seen since early July.

She approached smiling, her teeth ivory against a face that was suntanned and freckled. She was wearing clam-digger shorts and open sandals, her perfume faint and rich-smelling. Leaning her elbows on the car, she smacked gum while helping herself to a cigarette from my shirt pocket. Lighting it off the one I was smoking, she inhaled with a cough. She stood on her toes, then on her heels, then on the sides of her feet, as if to show me that all of these joints were working. When I reached to put a hand on her hip, she slapped it and stepped back. "Now you be nice!"

I told her I was on my way to the golf course.

She said, "Oh great. I'll follow and watch you tee off."

"Sure, if you like."

"Afterwards maybe we can hang out."

"Maybe, but I have to be getting back."

She went to the scooter and returned with a Titleist golf ball.

"I found this in the golf club parking lot," she grinned. "It's number seven for good luck."

"I could sure use some of that."

"I could walk around the course with you, caddy?"

I thought about this and told her no. She was not dressed properly and had not played the game so would get me into trouble with her lack of etiquette. I had organized a match with some guys from the mill. I told her that after the round I would take her to the Parker Hotel for a beer. She nodded and kissed me on the cheek before returning to her bike. I wondered if Tony, her old boyfriend, had ever come back into her life.

On the course, the scent of freshly cut grass was overpowering the river-smelling breeze. Through the trees, beyond the first tee the big river shimmered like a plate made of wrinkled chrome. I could hear the waves thrashing against the rocky shore, see the buildings rise above the water on the far side. Behind a hedge, on the street side of the fairway, was the ivy-covered stone clubhouse, a nineteenth-century mansion with green shutters and extended awnings, under which people sat in cloth chairs and read newspapers while having breakfast. It might have been a scene from early Hollywood. For a moment, my old dream of owning such a place came back to me. Wilma and I were in that house, preparing social events and arranging golf matches for the off hours. But at that point I hardly knew this young woman and realized she could be whoever I wanted her to be. I liked her for her still-unfamiliar self.

She stood in the parking lot and watched as I moved through the swing, ever so smoothly, my clubface making a "*crack*" on impact so the ninety-compression Titleist raised and hooked slightly down the right centre of the fairway. I heard her little applause. As I walked down number one, I listened to her scooter bleating in the street. She would be back to meet me after the round.

I had hit a decent drive, leaving only a short approach to the flat green. In my mind the golf lesson fundamentals of the swing repeated themselves. These I went over, whether at work or in bed in a state of non-sleep – a time when the swing was perfect, the score below par – and again at parties where I acted out the life of a golf professional.

"You see, ladies, perception is in the head, projection is in the hands, look good to be good. Think positive. Dress like a pro. Play anywhere with a good swing." *But slow down, David. You are never going to hit the ball like Gary Player!* These words from the golf instructor lived inside me as I played the game, worked at the mill, partied, or slept. There were times when, after hitting a long drive with a draw, I could feel greatness was near. It would all come together, I thought, with experience, more lessons, possibly as soon as next year. After all, I had gotten off to a late start. Having been born and raised in a youth home, I had a greater handicap than most. When it all came together, I would apply for a job at the pro shops. David Kelly, Assistant Pro. Wow! The title would lift me into a completely new circle, away from that loathsome poorhouse, and union, legacy.

I had heard them talking at the club. The pro was invited to dinner parties, spoke at Rotary luncheons, and was looked up to by the rich. A good swing and nice clothes would make up for a lot of shortfalls: the lack of an education, the blue-collar dogma, the institutional upbringing. Still, for the time being, I golfed with union members. I would register for more clinics in the fall.

When I finished my round this day, Wilma was waiting in the parking lot. She hopped into my car, eager to know how it went.

"The game of golf is like life – so much of it is in the mind," I told her.

"But you enjoyed yourself, that's the main thing."

At the Parker, the waiter would not serve Wilma because she had no ID, so we got pop and chips at a corner store, headed down the river road toward Point Cheval Beach. Along that winding road there were apple orchards surrounding the faded-brick farmhouses, their vine-clad verandas facing the river. In the parklands, families picnicked under the big trees. It was the closest thing I had seen to the old dream I had been nurturing, the lifestyle I so desired.

From a parking lot, a pathway curved to a stone bridge, arched over a gulch, and extended down to the shore. We would have privacy there. Once, my first love Paula – she was long married, sadly to a car salesman – and I had bathed here. We had built a fire on the shore, roasted wieners. Later, because I was drinking rum, I dragged an old car tire from the trees, threw it on the blaze. This filled the area with smoke and the smell of burning rubber, which brought park maintenance workers, firefighters, and cops. Not realizing that such things could not be done in this area, we hid in the woods.

Now, the shore was sandy and cool, the big river a sheet of glass with moving dimples. Here in the estuary, below the townships, branches of the weeping willow trees hung into the water. It reminded me of photos I had seen of the Amazon. But if you looked downriver you could see, above the treetops, the sparkling Atlantic Ocean. Sticky with sweat from the golf round, I took off my shirt, slacks, and socks before wading in. I felt the algae-covered rocks under my feet before getting down to swim against the slow-moving currents.

"C'mon in. It's not cold, not after you're in a while."

"I got no bathing suit."

"Neither do I!"

Dog-paddling, I caught sight of Wilma, bending to take off her shorts, her buttocks white in the bushes. She tiptoed over the sand and splashed into the water with a scream. She swam around me, one hell of a swimmer, before making swan dives and leg stretches and going down to sneak up beside me and pull me under. The water took my breath away. We waded onto the warm sand to lie under a weeping willow tree and smoke, while letting the breeze dry us. Wilma's hair strung down over her sunburned eyes like eel grass, her sandy pubis next to mine as in a dream.

I pulled her under me and we made love, tasting each other's tongues, the river, tanning lotion, tobacco smoke, Coke, and chips. And the passion that oozed from each other's pores.

"Good for you too?"

"Oh yes ... ooooh yessss."

There was no anger, no scarred knees or kicking heels to hold one back. (Not like it had been with Paula.) This was tender but energetic, giving both ways, with some hurried breathing, followed by a long embrace. No unwantedness meant no guilt, no tears, no peeing oneself in the night afterward. The fear, if there was any, came out of not knowing Wilma's age. She might have been nineteen or thirty-five. She would not say, and was not the least concerned.

"Let's just enjoy *this* day for what it is," she said.

That was my philosophy too.

Still, all enjoyable things were scary to me, especially if they came too easy. Sister Connors, a nun from Saint Peters who used to visit the youth home, told me that sexual pleasures exact a high price and that we pay with sorrow for every enjoyable minute we relish from them. I wondered why something so beautiful was not meant to be enjoyed. Were we not allowed to follow our hearts, as in dreams? Being there with Wilma had been a real-life enactment of all my youthful fantasies. And just as magic. It was an untangling of frustrations, a flesh-and-blood example of how things should be.

We stretched out on the sand and dozed off. Then we went for another dip, dressed, and I drove back into town. Relaxed and confident, I changed into street clothes and in the heat of the afternoon headed down the King's Highway to horse races in Kingsbury. The song "Marie" was playing on the radio as I breathed in the warm convertible winds.

* * *

The October day was breezy with leaves dropping from the big trees along Albert Street, the sidewalks littered with willow sprouts. As I sat drinking tea on the veranda, the postman stopped with registered mail. I signed the form and opened the envelope, which contained a hand-written letter from Wilma. She said she needed to see me right away. See me? I wondered what she was up to. Why register a letter? I phoned her house, and when she answered, at first I did not recognize her voice.

"David, where [cough] have you been?" She sounded depressed and hoarse, as if she had been smoking or drinking too much.

I took the ten minutes' drive upriver to Smith Falls.

When I pulled into her driveway, she ran out and jumped into the car beside me. She wore a trench coat with its belt drawn tight. Her hair had been cut and curled, her lips were faded, the blue veins in her temples obvious. She huddled close, while taking a cigarette from my shirt pocket and lighting it with trembling hands. When she shivered, I turned on the heater. It was not a cold day and I wondered if she had a nervous condition. Or was I seeing her for the first time when I was actually sober?

As we drove down King's Highway past the closed-up Court House Theatre and the median's shuttered town clock and bandstand, there was no one on the sidewalks, the quaint old town of Point Cheval having withdrawn into itself for the winter. And there were no vehicles on the leaf-littered River Road, with its curves outlined with yellow crayon.

Wilma remained silent, although I could hear her deep sighs.

At Point Cheval Beach, I drove into a parking lot and we got out and walked toward the river. It was the place we had come to swim last summer. Now, I could glimpse the tar-coloured water just beyond the yellow foliage. The cool breeze made the big river raw and uninviting, the sea beyond, a speckled black. We sat on a park bench in the lee of the stone bridge and smoked. I asked her about the letter.

She ignored my question. Instead she talked about the day we went there after golf and swam and made love.

"And why couldn't we do more of that kind of thing together?"

Her hand with the lit cigarette trembled as she stared at the ground, as though seeing that summer's day as a time of magic, a period already gone from her world. Or perhaps she had a hangover and was fighting a severe state of melancholy. I was battling this too, as I always did in the fall. For a second, she reminded me of me, the way she hung onto a special little moment from the past. And

I wondered if she was also struggling with aloneness, that blue time of year. I put a hand on her shoulder and gave a squeeze. "Willie, come back to the apartment with me. We'll have a beer, hang out."

She did not respond; rather she sat with her head down. She made a groove in the sand with the side of her shoe, covered it over, and then she made it again. Finally, taking my hands in hers, she looked into my eyes and with a glassy stare said, "David, I'm pregnant!"

And she started to bawl.

I wrapped my arms around her. I had never been able to see someone cry without shedding a tear myself.

"Oh, Wilma."

She wiped her eyes and blew her nose, before tucking the handkerchief into the sleeve of her coat. She did not speak, just stared. And I was afraid to pry into her affairs.

"But do you know for sure?"

"Oh, yes, I know," she said, looking away.

"And the father, does he know?"

"Yes, Tony knows. He's the one I've been sleeping with a long time now."

"And me, last summer!"

"And you, last summer!" She kept staring at the ground. Her hands appeared to be in kinks as she twisted them every which way.

"But why isn't Tony here now when you need him for support?"

"David, he can't be here." She looked at me over the wing-shaped collar of her trench coat. "Tony is married already." Her voice cracked, as if the name Tony stirred a deeper emotion, one more dramatic than the pregnancy.

She stood up, tugged her hair, and paced back and forth. For an instant, I thought of Sister Connors' words about everything enjoyable coming with a price.

"But how could you – I mean, how could he?"

"I know it shouldn't have happened with him being married and all, but ... David, you know I love you a whole bunch too!"

"If that's the kind of guy he is, you're better off without him anyway. But what can I do about any of this?" I glanced at her stomach, which was flat as a board.

"You were the only one I felt I could talk to. You've gone through a lot yourself and I figured you would understand. I thought maybe you would –"

I interrupted, "But how do you know you're really pregnant? Can you be sure?"

"C'mon, David, how does anyone know? I mean, I can tell ..."

I fumbled for something to smoke even though I was smoking already.

"Have you been to a doctor?"

"Not yet."

"Then you have to go."

"I know. But I'm scared of what she'll tell me," Wilma whispered like a child sharing a secret. Her lips quivered like she was going to cry again.

"I'll go with you!"

"Can't do that."

"Do your parents know?"

"David, I can't tell them. They would kick me out of the house. And I can't afford a place right now."

"But you're a grown woman. Would they not understand?"

"You don't know my parents. We are an old Swedish family. This would be a disgrace. They would kick me out of the will and the family."

"Oh, sweet Jesus!" I felt a shortness of breath and coughed.

"Are you choking up?" she asked in a calm, low tone.

"I'm okay. Don't worry about me." I grasped her sleeve. "Wilma, we have to give this some serious thought."

"We don't have much time."

"Yes we do! We have all the time we want."

"I suppose there's one thing we can do." She looked away.

"What's that?"

"Get married! You and me."

"Whhaaaaaatt!"

"Well, why not! Do you want my baby to be raised in an institution like you were?"

"No goddamn way," I said. "But I don't want to be pushed into a marriage either. Not this way, especially when it's Tony's child."

"What would the difference be? Maybe we could make it work." When she said this, she squeezed my hands, her voice lightened, and she gave me a faint smile, her freckles almost invisible.

"But you don't love me, you love Tony. And I'd always be wondering if you would go back to him if you got the chance."

"Dave, I'll give you my word of honour that I won't do that. I hate the bastard right now."

"But, Wilma, look at me. You can do better than this. Don't feel pressured to marry just anyone at all. I am a piece of garbage. You must not have anything to do with me. I'm not good for you. I'm not good for anyone. I was brought up in a youth home, everybody knows that!"

"You're not garbage!" she cried. "Don't put yourself down that way. You're a soul person who says exactly what you think. And you are lacking the attention you deserve too. I heard you say 'I love you' to me when you were sleeping. If I didn't think you were a good person, I wouldn't ask you to marry me. Maybe we could be good together. We had some good times last summer. We could raise the baby and it would be ours, yours and mine. I mean, who would know the difference?"

"Wilma, I'm a heap a trash, I tell you. The only thing I could give you is a lot of heartaches and troubles! I mean, I have problems you don't know about – hang-ups and scars and all kinds of bad habits that go way back. I'm an alcoholic, I have asthma and ..."

"Asthma is caused by allergies, we all have allergies. Do you want me to go to Children's Aid, talk to them about giving the baby over for adoption?"

"No! Whatever you do, don't go to those child welfare people about anything."

I was getting irritated because of the way Wilma was pressuring me. "Tell me you won't go to anyone but the doctor! What do these people know about you and me and Tony and what we have done and what we would like to do? What do counsellors know about what goes on inside another person's head, and what they have gone through? It's like going to a priest for advice on marriage!

I've had my fill of quacks at the detention centre. And don't these people deal with children's pregnancies? How old are you?"

"They deal with any pregnancy. I'm twenty-five!"

"Really? And here I thought ... So at our ages shouldn't we know more about us than some counsellor?"

"Oh, David, I know we should. So can you help me figure it out?"

"First, we have to find out for sure."

"You could help me start my period."

"How?"

"Slippery elm stick."

"No goddamn way! People die from that. You would be dead and I would be charged with manslaughter!"

"Then?"

"You have to go to a doctor!"

"Okay. I'll go, I'll go," she said, and appeared to lighten up.

As I drove Wilma home, she had tears in her eyes, a baby in her belly. She was smoking, non-stop. It had started to rain, big silver drops bouncing off the canvas roof, glazing the windshield when I turned the wipers on so that I could barely see the road. Hailstones hopped into the roadside grass, while red and yellow leaves boiled up behind the car to fall again and stick to the greasy pavement.

"Call me." I gave her sleeve a tug as she got out of the car. "Let me know how it goes!"

"I will." She gave me a faint smile, slammed the door, and ran. The tails of her trench coat were flapping against her white ankles.

"I can get my hands on money," I hollered. But she had already gone inside.

As I drove back to Albert Street, I thought, that woman doesn't really know who I am. She knows only what she has seen at parties and that was mostly an act. And I would not be forced into something I didn't think would work out, for either of us. She didn't know it, but she would be better off alone than having me for a husband. Tony was the one she loved. She had told me many times in many different ways.

But neither would I see her baby grow up in an institution like I did. Or for that matter Tony's and Wilma's child either; no one in my circle was going to grow up in a welfare house as long as I was able to work at the mill, provide a home. I just would not let it happen. I wondered if Wilma would get an abortion, if I paid for it. What would a doctor give her for advice? I thought, maybe I should see a counsellor, now finally tell her all about my association with Paula – a relationship with a ghost from the youth home years – and Wilma, who was now looking for a father for her would-be illegitimate child. I wanted a family? Now I had one for the taking. I drove all afternoon, turning it over in my mind.

I decided I would pay whatever it cost to support Wilma's child. I would work nights in the mill forever to keep it from an institution. I would quit drinking, quit smoking, quit golfing, quit playing the horses, give up all my addictions ... And if I kept straight and Wilma wanted to marry me when she got to know me better, we could do it ...

In truth, after I thought about it, I got excited about raising a son or a daughter even if it was not my own blood. Especially if it was not my blood, but something better. For sure there had been no blood relations at the youth home. And if I could push Paula out of the picture, my love for Wilma would come, I was sure of it. I felt that I could push Tony out of the picture too, because he had not been loyal to his wife, nor had he been there for Wilma when she needed him most. I knew enough mill workers like that to fill a passenger train. They huddled on the outer edges of humanity, drank cheap draught beer at the hotels, were protected by the union brotherhood, and took responsibility for nothing. Besides, I had feelings for Wilma, and I felt this could be nurtured. But I would not go to anyone for advice on this one. It was my decision, mine and Wilma's. Like Paula used to say, "I had gone to the river to meditate, and this was my resolve."

Push Paula out of the picture? Ah, yes, had I forgotten? She had gone from my world years ago. And now, this was the real thing. This was life in its truest form. The old dreams of escaping the mill, becoming a golf professional, owning a vine-covered inn, the show business act if I made it at the races were out of reach and appeared to be frivolous. And down deep, I guess I knew they always had been. (Although, where I came from, the so-called institution, they were all the dreams I could have.) Yes, it had all been an act to help cover my shortfalls. Those superficial lifestyles, the fool's paradise would be all too unpredictable for a man with responsibilities, a family man. I could see myself as a union worker for the rest of my life. And that would be okay because for once I was taking responsibility, thinking of someone other than myself. I wanted a family; now I had one.

Still, in the back of my mind, because I did not know this young woman well, I could picture myself in a troubled relationship that could lead to a broken home, a fatherless child, all because we had married for the wrong reasons. I never doubted that Wilma would not go back to Tony, even though, every time she looked at the baby, she would see his face. But as I said many times, we can love more than one person and it doesn't always have to be two ways. Wilma and I were both in love with someone else. And it was this hodgepodge of feelings that I wrestled with.

I did not hear from Wilma, although I tried to reach her many times, even the next day, to tell her I had decided to support the child, even marry her, if that was what it took to keep the baby from an institution. Not until a foggy evening in late October, when I drove to Smith Falls, did I catch her home. When I pulled into her driveway and honked, she ran out and jumped into the car. She acted like her old self, bouncy and full of fun. She lit a cigarette from my pack while she fumbled with the radio dial.

"Wilma, I love you! You are the best!"

"No. Don't, don't ..."

She looked at me kind of silly like. She grinned, and her teeth were white as chalk. Finally, she said, "David, I'm not pregnant. You don't have to marry me and you don't have to love me, so there, you're free to go."

Her words lifted a heavy burden, and for a brief moment, I felt giddy and wanted to laugh too. And then I wanted to cry, because I had so thoughtfully laid out my whole life with and around her and the baby. It was a future that was more realistic than any I had ever dreamed of before.

"Really?"

"Yes, my period started. The doctor said I'm okay."

"Look, down the road a ways, maybe we could get together and ..."

"No, no," she interrupted. "Don't worry about it! That's all behind me now. It's behind you too."

I wanted to cry. Because I felt I could have done more in the crisis, and with a lot more dignity. This was followed by the image of a son or a daughter who called *me* daddy, slipping out of view, the little stucco home in Point Cheval disappearing. I tried not to speak, because I did not feel worthy of saying anything. And I knew I could not talk without crying. But I felt good for her in that she now had her freedom. And no one would ever know I had been willing to marry a woman I was not sure I could love, really love, and father a child that was not mine, really mine: no one but me and that little man who sang and danced in front of a big mirror at the apartment on Albert Street, after just two drinks.

"Wilma, I'm glad," I said. "I am glad for you."

I was going to tell her what I had decided to do, but thought better of it. Why try to be a hero now?

"Yeah, me too."

Instead I said, "Wilma, I don't really know what I want. I guess, deep down, I'm trying to nurture a dream that just won't go away. It's a dream to be someone who I never will be. And I am not really capable of making a big decision, maybe I never have been, especially when it affects someone else's life in the way this would have yours."

"You seem to be caught somewhere in the past." She gave me a smirk. "And sometimes you call me Paula. Who the hell is Paula?"

"Just someone I knew years ago at the home. I have a lot of old scars."

"David, we can't really wait for dreams to come true. This is real life. Perfection comes only in our imaginations."

"I know. Someone I respect told me I need counselling, family enhancement. You are really better off without me, you know."

"And you're not garbage." She smiled. "Don't think that for a minute. Anyone who cries over another person's hurt is not bad. And I know that you would have given up your dream to keep my baby out of an institution. I could feel the concern you had for me."

These were kind words that made me feel better. I took a deep breath. I thought, from now on I will not mess with people's feelings, as I have been messed with all my life.

After that visit, I did not hear from Wilma. I wanted to call, but thought, it's better for her if I stay out of her life.

Then, just a few days before Christmas, I got a call from Mrs. Johansson, Wilma's mother, who had found my name and phone number in her daughter's things. When I asked about Wilma, she said that she was surprised I had not read the news in *The Times*; that in late November, Wilma had jumped over Smith Falls and had drowned. She whispered, "Willie was four months pregnant at the time of her death."

The Burial

On an August Sunday, late morning when the sun was yellowing, and at the window an autumnal chill was on the breeze, I got out of bed, dressed, had breakfast, and walked down along the riverbank and across the wire bridge to visit Archie Long, my old friend who always had a full pack of cigarettes. As I crossed the shaky spans, I looked down into the water to see many big salmon lying in the shadows of the middle abutment. This was a scene that would normally have me going back to the house for my angling gear. But I was not into fishing this day; I was in love, and people who are in love are seldom responsive to the beauties of nature. I was fascinated with Carolyn Wood, a young woman from the village I had met just two weeks before.

At first, I had walked with her along the village sidewalks, always revealing my best side, before seeing her home and kissing her goodnight. And then the next evening, when I was sitting in the back seat of my father's car that was parked on Main Street, I saw Carolyn coming down the sidewalk. She was wearing a long plaid coat, then all the rage, a white scarf, and black oxford shoes. When she saw me, she came right over, opened the door, jumped in, and gave me a hug. We embraced and kissed and rolled about on the seat in a passionate exchange that steamed up the windows. Shy by nature, it was the most obsessive squeeze I had experienced to that point in my life. We romped about, until Papa came back to the car from a meeting he had been attending and wanted to go home.

So Carolyn and I got out and walked together about the village: in and out of diners, into the old movie house and the pool hall where we listened to music on a nickelodeon – Elvis Presley's "Don't Be Cruel" and Buddy Holly's "That'll Be the Day," melodies that would bring back the moment when I heard them on the radio sixty years later. It was nice to be seen hanging out with such a beautiful woman, although Papa never liked the Wood family and cautioned me about befriending Carolyn. "She's a yuppie," he told me. "You'll always be at her disposal." Still, in the Railroad Station, Carolyn and I embraced and I whispered in her ear that I loved her, before walking with her down Main Street where I kissed her goodnight on her mother's front veranda.

The next weekend, having been able to borrow Papa's car, I picked Carolyn up at her house and we drove through the village many times – I wanted to show her off – eventually ending up behind the Boy Scout Hall where we parked in a wooded area and I smothered her with kisses. We were on the verge of sex – I was at arm's length of encountering those unknown pleasures – when we were interrupted by the village police officer, who aimed a flashlight into our eyes and told us to move along, go to our homes and go to bed!

By then, I already knew that I was in love with the dark-eyed, curly-haired woman and that I would never get the same thrill out of fishing or hunting or just horsing around with my outlandish buddies again. I had outgrown them and had become a new person in just two weeks. It was a high that I never experienced before, a state of bliss that carried me, like a dream, right through the hours and days. She was with me when I walked in the balsam-and-thyme-scented woods. She was with me at evening in the yellow fields of corn stook when the purple rays of the setting sun reflected through birch trees on the riverbank, a time of day when feelings of aloneness overtook me. Or when I went boating on the river. Indeed, Carolyn Wood was present in everything I did. I told this to Archie as we lay on the ground – we were well back from his barn with its mows filled with new hay – a lawn that had been kept mowed close to the roots by his two strawberry roan horses, and smoked his tobacco.

Archie, now a middle-aged bachelor, though well grounded, had had these feelings long before, had loved and lost, and had learned to live without a woman in his life. He told me to pursue her to the fullest, not to let her get away, but also that she would not be easy to maintain, with her coming from town and me being a farm boy. "You wouldn't have much in common outside of the physical attractions," he told me.

That was the barrier that he figured had cost him his love so long before. For me, the idea of losing my first love was a discouraging thought and I wanted more than ever to measure up to her standards, her expectations of me. I was in love, and Carolyn Wood suddenly figured into everything I had ever dreamed of doing. I pined for her when we were apart, but kept from calling her house as I did not want to appear to be overeager. I soon found out that one cannot love without a degree of suffering, and that we have to endure some pain before we can apprehend truth. Such are the dreams and the sadness of youth.

Finally, I left Archie and walked back across the shaky cable bridge and up through the oat-stubble fields to home. When I got to our house, I found that Carolyn had been there to visit *me*. My high school friend, Nick Dolan, had been out driving and had picked up Carolyn and her friend Shirley Keenan and had taken it upon himself to drive that five-mile stretch of gravel road from the village to our farm. Finding that I was on the other side of the river, they had walked out on the bridge, took photos of each other standing against the cables, and then Nick had taken the girls back to the village.

When I found this out I was disappointed that I had not been home to greet them, but I was also frustrated with Nick for the reason that he had done this, on impulse, without warning me, because our road was gravelled and rutty – it would have looked so much nicer under a covering of snow in late fall or early winter when I had planned to bring her here – and our farmyard was shabby, with hens and calves feeding around the back door, undergarments hanging on the clothesline. And everyone, except Papa and Mamma, who always dressed up on Sundays, would have been in everyday flannel and denim work clothes. Without anyone having had a chance to prepare for her, she would have seen the very worst side of my home and family.

Because of these humble origins, I wondered if the visit would put a stop to my relationship with this beautiful town-bred woman. Because our bond was so fragile, I felt that maybe our love was not that strong and that a lot of what I had been dreaming of was in *my* mind only. I wondered if her seeing my old home place, so crude in comparison to her town house, before she had time to fall seriously in love with me, would end things forever. Certainly whatever opinion she had of me until then would have lessened with her visit here, although I was proud of my relations, especially Mamma and Papa. I was drunk with rage and lovesickness.

I also wondered if Nick had done this on purpose to try to destroy Carolyn's and my relationship. This sometimes happens with country lads when they see one of their own moving up the social ladder past them. I knew too that if the affair fell through, I would never find contentment again. Having tasted the upper crust of society, the conversation of which I sometimes grasped to comprehend – it meant that I was growing – the passions of a deep kiss, though ever-so-briefly, feeling her heart beat so close to mine, I would never be able to rediscover the old innocence of adolescence, those happy days of wandering about the fields and river without a care or a serious dream.

I changed into my town clothes, borrowed my father's car, and drove that gravel road, up and down the long hills, cutting close around sharp bends that made the fenders pop, leaving behind me a five-mile cloud of dust to drift away in the winds, out over the browning fields and the tea-stained river, to lodge in the tree branches of a jagged horizon. I looked for Carolyn in the diners and the pool hall but she was not to be seen in the now vacated village.

On the following Saturday, for it was on this night that us country lads tried to make things happen, I dressed in my best denim jeans and sports shirt and walked to the village, hopping into the woods at the approach of a car that would fill my world with dust and hold me to the bottom rung of the social ladder. Again I looked for Carolyn but she was not around. When I asked Nick if he had seen her, he told me that she had gone to the city where she had an uncle and that she would be gone for some time. At first I thought that she might write to me, explain the circumstances that had been beyond her control, apologize for not filling me in, and perhaps ask for reconciliation. I checked the post office daily, but each time I went there I was more disappointed. I wondered if I would ever see my sweetheart again, realizing that my memories of her would haunt me for a lifetime.

In the village on Saturday nights, I looked for her, and the distance between us grew through the passage of time, which was invisible to me as I was at a standstill. I carried her love inside me like a virus. On the jukebox, I played the country song "I Still Care." And I felt the hurt in the voice of the singer. This was more than a song, it was an experience. (They say that all you need to write a good country song is three chords, truth, and a whole lot of lonesome. For sure I felt that I could have written a hit tune that autumn.) After a while I was ashamed to be seen alone in the diners, answering questions: Where's your lover tonight? How is Carolyn? Where did she go? You see, unable to contain my pleasures of loving her, I had bragged to my friends about the relationship. Now that she was gone, I stayed at home on weekends and wept in silence. Sadly, one day my lover just went away and she never came back.

Later, I learned from Shirley Keenan that Carolyn had, in fact, moved to the city of Toronto. I figured that our little love affair, though earth-moving to me, for her had been a teen crush and nothing more. Lonely country boys, who see a threat behind every door, take things like acceptance more seriously than townspeople do. I realized this before I had a chance to enjoy the budding April cruelties: the heated passions of sex, the augmented different philosophies, town and country, to bathe together in the hot river water of summer. Autumn had arrived prematurely and I could see a deplorable long winter on the horizon, her leaving having shaped my destiny.

After Carolyn was gone from my life for some time, I tried to go back to my old lifestyle: fishing in the mornings, gardening in the afternoons, hunting in the evenings, or just hanging out with my buddies in the village on Saturday nights. But having experienced love, having been lifted to new heights of passion, indeed a higher dimensional dream, my heart was not into it and I was bored with the ones who had not experienced the pleasure and did not know the territory, or perhaps they did know it, and like me, were unsuccessful and trying to adapt to the different circumstance, back into the old confinement, each of us playing a different instrument to a different soul music.

And I thought that the woman we do not know is always more true and lovable than the one we know, the one who does not know us. For in the end it is our own instincts that we react to. Why hang out with losers? I thought. It was a boring, dark zone that would leave me working the farm, with no dreams now, but memories, trying to enjoy the pleasures of the mind, like my friend Archie who had become a stubborn recluse. For sure it was no place for a sentimentalist who was hypersensitive and was now suffering from deep heart wounds, so that I could no longer enjoy the familiar sounds of the wind in the chimney, the whisper of a pine tree, the pungent odours of the swamp, the sight of the soft melting snowflakes.

It was right after high school graduation that I left the country on a Greyhound bus, got an apartment in Toronto, and set out to study music at the Royal Conservatory.

But I found the big city to be cold and loveless, with an overpowering sense of commerce. Walking in the bohemian quarter, I tried to block out the voices of the marketers and the sharks in trade.

"Step right up! Hot dogs, hamburgers, french fries for a dollar!"

And there was the circus music from the rushing ambulances and police sirens, of car horns that were in harmony with the overtures of tinkling doorbells, the hissing of air brakes, the clatter of the milkman's shoes on the cobbled sidewalks, the echoes in a symphony of train whistles. Rather I listened to the fiddle within: the music of water on a spring morning on the river Cains while tenting with Papa; of a blue jay's cry from God's country, Morse Brook; of the Friday afternoon concerts after a long school week, the sweet grade five voices in song; of the crackle and snap of an autumn bonfire at the lake; the scent of Papa's freshly lit pipe; the taste of Mamma's homemade blueberry pie and ice cream; of stewed currants, still warm in a jar. These reflections were the only peace of mind that I could find.

"Step this way! Salmon and shad, fresh off the boat!"

Sometimes the street sounds would jolt me back to beautiful but painful sensations, memories I both treasured and tried to avoid, like Carolyn's sweet breathing in my ear in the back seat of Papa's car so long before. I looked for and sometimes glimpsed her in crowds. Once I spotted her at the Royal Alex, in a black dress and pearls, though perhaps a bit taller and slimmer. She was sitting beside a gray-haired man in a black suit. We were watching The Royal Winnipeg Ballet perform *The Nutcracker*. Why did I think she would be there?

Later I saw her on the subway, though briefly. She was wearing shorts and sandals and looking very much like Ava Gardner, tall and stately, standing head and shoulders above the others who appeared to be admiring her as well.

A decade later we made love on an airplane, in the middle of the night, somewhere between Calgary and Toronto. With her mother asleep on the adjacent seat, she had put her beautiful hand, with the pink nails, back into my air space. Yes, we were riding the Red Eye in the friendly skies of Air Canada. Or had it been someone who resembled Jill Anderson, my dear grade eight friend, in a plaid skirt, away back, a hand stroke, a leg that resembled hers, in pantyhose? Such is the cruelty, the sweet sadness of memory. It could have been anyone within the boundaries of my lasting and now lying memory and vision of her. It was a risky business, and for a time I did not know if my nerves would stand it, the physical exercise having overpowered any degree of common sense.

And there was her portrait that hung in the lobby of Massey Hall. In a white formal dress, she had gracefully developed a countenance of good lines; her eyes were bright and sincere, her mouth well formed, without anger, her brow smooth like an artist's, the nose fine and straight. What eyes, I thought. What class. Since my youth, I had secretly loved her, having gone through my own awkward stages into maturity, the teen, the indifferent youth, and the abstract, reticent man. Generally it would take more than six women to bring so many changes to a person's progression.

Later that summer, during a thunderstorm, we showered together under the eaves of my farmhouse – now a cottage – with the rain coming straight down in troughs to spill around our feet and make the buildings and picket fences glisten as if they had been polished with varnish. There had been times, inspired by a smell or a taste, when she came to me, though briefly, and in the clothes I had last seen her in – or perhaps, after long periods of aloneness, no clothes at all.

Years later I returned from Ontario and made a career of teaching music at Mount Allison University in Sackville, New Brunswick.

* * *

And then, after sixty-odd years had passed, and the winds of winter were in the air, Carolyn Wood came back to the village to bury her mother's ashes in the old local cemetery. Home on a holiday, I wondered if I should go to the reception, and if she would remember me, child-minded as I was when I knew her, but now suffering from an old man's delusions. Or if she would actually want to reacquaint with someone who now had two chins, sagging red eyes, a virago's nose, and a single remaining tuft of hair that resembled a hazelnut burr. But I thought, at this age, what do I have to lose by going? What do I have to gain by not going? Two years older than Carolyn, I imagined that I might look to her like Papa did to me before he died in the winter of '72.

Walking about the now indifferent village street, a location that had once been the social centre of my universe, I found that the place was filled with ghosts, inspired perhaps by the atmosphere on a crumbling sidewalk or around some old closed-up building, made more forlorn by a lonesome train whistle or the knell from a distant church spire. The local people I met appeared to have a sense of defeatism, a feature externalized by their slow gait and bad posture. These things were made more forsaken by a dark cloud covering and with a light rain falling, the houses glowing at various windows. But everything was being overshadowed by the possibility of seeing Carolyn Wood.

Through the years, from her memory, a sense of melancholy struck me harder on days like this, or on those late fall evenings, the cool woods and quiet fields, the sky lonely with its soft-melting snowflakes coming down while I sat at the piano with a promising student, going over the scales, plunking out a sonata or a quartet, perhaps Chopin's *Polonaise in E Flat Major* or Schubert's *Fantasia in F Minor*, the colour tones of which led my emotions back to Carolyn, or perhaps a school song we had sung in the old days, a tune we had shared from on the car radio. This, even though I had not laid eyes on her in over fifty years.

At the cemetery, because I am not a religious person, I stood well back, out of earshot of the minster's words, the rain dappling my fall coat.

After the burial, in the church hall, everyone was served ham sandwiches and date squares with decaffeinated tea and coffee in paper cups. The men were dressed in dark suits, some wearing black wigs – this made them look older – and thick glasses. The women, without jewellery, were wearing black dresses, their silver hair glistening under the lights. And there were pockets of perfumes drifting about the room. From the stir, these pockets mixed to make a potion of incestuous homogeny. Looking about the crowded hall, I spotted a woman who could be Carolyn.

Yes, it was her aquiline nose, though somewhat larger from how I remembered it. She was sitting among, and in conversation with, some elderly women. I made my way toward her for the meeting that I had so long desired. We had so much catching up to do. From the years, her face had turned dark and crisp, like the pages of an old book, dark pencilled eyebrows being her autumnal fashion. In fact, she was so far from that youthful image I had been carrying inside myself all the years, I was sorry I had come. She would have been better left buried in the distant, romantic past and under the safeguard of nostalgia. For, as an escape, my mind still carried in it the cinema of a much earlier day. And I suddenly realized that nothing is as painful as the contradicting of memory, the melancholy of youth having been destroyed, so that I was now looking at her mother.

Indeed, Mrs. Wood's characteristics had taken over the daughter's younger face. And her worst features were exaggerated out of all proportion. Certain faces have a better power of survival than others, stand up through time and do not change with the approach of the metaphoric winter of life, especially the chin, which in her case had multiplied threefold and was mottled like a windfall apple. Recalling my old-time religious superstitions, I wondered if the spirit of her mother prevailed in the room and that after forty days of requiem we could sing her into the great beyond. But Carolyn was no less her mother than I was my father, both of whom had been old antagonists, the years or perhaps our attitudes and philosophic growth appearing to have destroyed any reflective narrative from our times together.

Gone too now was the thrill of dreaming of what might have been, the narrative that had been playing inside me for all that time. Her appearance brought forth memories of her mother, a woman who, in times gone by, I had also found to be arrogant. These connotations also existed in her contemporaries, whose numbers would have been diminishing by the day. These were the so-called dignitaries of the village: the mayor and his bejewelled wife, the barber and his century-old mother, the original storekeeper at the Save Easy, the clerk at the Credit Union, the attendant at the service station – hardly blue-blooded aristocrats or members of the Harvard Club – and some of her mother's relatives, one of whom, by his own admission, was a pianist. This well-dressed man, who, immediately upon entering the room treated me with indifference, sat down at the keyboard and started plunking on the middle C. People were leaning on their canes and chatting. And there were anemic pockets of laughter. One small group was admiring Mrs. Wood's pencil sketch of Sir Winston Churchill, with the balding head and cigar, both of which I found to be disproportionate to his shoulders and arms. And I thought, there is great nobility in the arts, so why not give it a try. It communicates its powers or lack thereof to any person who criticizes it. Someone said, "Oh, how nice! Gloria had such talent."

I thought, these are the society people I respected, even feared in my youth, with Carolyn among them. They approached the piano, which was being played by ear and off-key – it was not like the piece of music was complicated, or a masterpiece that was really new and needed study – and stood around it to sing Mrs. Wood's favourite hymn, "Take Me Home, Sweet Jesus."

After the singing, I whispered to the would-be pianist, whose hair was thin like the whiskers on a corncob, "Buddy, you not only need practice, you need lessons! But the fiddler must be paid." I tossed a two-dollar coin into an ashtray on the piano and chuckled to make it appear like I was joking. At which point he got up from the piano, slammed down the cover, and walked away, as though he was disgusted with me. This did not offend me in the least. "Nice tie, though," I called after him laughingly. And

I thought that only marriage problems could account for the bitterness I could see on his face.

I wanted to ask Carolyn why she had skipped away, so long ago, without so much as saying goodbye. But when I introduced myself to her and kissed her hand, a hand that had blue veins pencilled from the onset of seventy-odd years, she did not remember or pretended not to remember who I was. She smiled in a cordial fashion, a show of courtesy to a total stranger. In truth I did not know this woman either, or perhaps never did. So the two seniors that we had become, devoid of reality, both hard of hearing and sight, both suffering from dementia in a noisy room, attempted to reacquaint. We spoke, mask to mask.

"Carolyn, do you remember the night we parked in the woods behind the Scout camp and and we sort of made out and cops came and we … ?"

There was an intangible look on her face. Finally, she spoke. "I can't remember ever seeing you before in my life," she said. "I believe you must be mistaking me for someone else." And she walked away to stand with some of her elderly female cousins.

For an instant I felt the same rejection I had suffered six decades before. I took a moment to regain my composure. At first I wanted to go after her, explain again the things she had failed to remember. But a feeling stronger than my own obliged me to finally turn my back on this woman forever. And for a brief moment I longed for a new impression, new sentiment to fill the void.

There was no hope of reconciliation, nor did I want there to be. This was the woman who betrayed me so long before, the woman whom I had not ceased to love. And suddenly I wondered how susceptible she was to other women and if that was her reason for abandoning me. I now realized that she had aged, but not matured, intellect having abandoned her physical growth, and then through the decline of a care-worn mind, her mother's arrogance had prevailed in her. By this time I was simply looking for truth. I walked away, vexed but not unhappy. Because I knew that if I tried to make contact with her again, explain the ghost, she would probably preach to me as I have had counsellors do.

I realized that the things I had once thought to be romantic and lovable – walking about the village with this woman on my arm, taking her to dances or a picture show, now with the beauty and indeed the spirit stripped from her person, and also from my person – appeared to me as foolery. Because when we are old, our one-time spirited bodies, our appearances and movements, fast or slow, witty or sad, do not matter. All frailties are overlooked as we search for someone in the group who still has some intellectual curiosity. Such is the maturity or immaturity, or even cynicism, of old age, after a long life of indifference to society itself. I now believe there to be a certain degree of arrogance and anger that befalls everyone in their declining years.

I went back to my cottage somewhat relieved that I did not have to put up with this conceited old woman who had captured my heart so long ago, and in memory I had so admired. It was a peace of mind I had not encountered in decades, having so often suffered the assault of memory at intervals through the years – on a blue Monday perhaps, during a sad autumn rainfall or a blizzard which conceivably prevented my recovery for days. I was glad too that she did not have to put up with me, as I was now set in a lifelong routine, my studies of the piano classics. She had abandoned me so that she could pursue her own agenda, her own kind of passion, in the big city, chase the destination of empowerment, and grow into the selfish person she had always been, even expand upon, but now with a demented state of simplicity. It would never work.

I finally realized how easy it would now be to forget her. And wished I could have made contact with the real Carolyn years before, so that I could have buried the past. For sure she was someone whom I had not seen clearly so long ago, in the nuance and haze of youth, those yellow days of summer and the new-found passions of adolescence, a time when I said my prayers and got into bed to dream only of her. She had been worth more as a symbol, the pleasant, though painful memory of first love, the passion and then later the apathy, than she was in reality. And I wondered how soon she would be heading back to the Big Smoke.

Our December Guest

On a blustery morning in early winter, there were snowflakes drifting past our frosted windows. As we huddled around the kitchen range, we could hear the snapping and cracking of the elm trees and the trail-bushed river ice so near our house. The fire having just been lighted, the kitchen was still cold as Papa and I faced the panting stove where tea was brewing. The kettle made a rustic sound like an axe being held to a grindstone, and there was the pungent odour of buckwheat pancakes that my mother was preparing. While my face was overheated from the fire, my back was chilled – indeed a wintery farmhouse atmosphere of long ago.

Father was telling his night's dream about a beggar man who came to our house from off the railway line. He was a Leonardo caricature, shabbily dressed, with a small pack and mystery in his eyes, a symbol of hard times and winter woes. This was a figure that Papa had often dreamed of on winter nights, an abstract man that only hand-screen art could recapture, a person who varied only by the effect of light or shade that changed due to the severity of the weather. Papa was telling Mamma and me this dream in sequence with the bitter morning noises, when a sharp knock came to the outside kitchen door. Kicking aside an old overcoat that had been thrown at the jamb to cut down the draft, Papa snapped the door open. There, in our outside shed, stood a figure that was an image of the man in his dreams. It was as though he had had a premonition or a fortune-teller had come to my father in the night and told him of the events that would follow. Though appearing to be in a state of shock, Papa said to him, "Come in, sir!"

The old man entered our kitchen and, trembling, made his way toward the stove, while Mamma poured him a mug of hot tea. He shivered and his teeth chattered as he sipped the brew without speaking. There was a coldness vibrating from his person, his nose and cheeks a red hue. He seemed to be caught in a daydream, as though he had regrets of a life wasted, or perhaps he felt indifferent to society, even our small family, and was ashamed of his predicament. He stood warming his hands – they were as black as coal – by rubbing them together above the stove's covers. Later, as he cleaned them at the washstand, I observed, as a boy filled with curiosity will, that one of his boots had a big gash in the side and that his thin suit coat was unravelled at the armpits. Where was he from, I wondered, and how did he end up so poor?

Eventually he spoke. "Thank 'e," he said, and held his cup out to Mamma for more tea. When Papa questioned him as to his mission, he said, in spurts and with a French accent, that he was on his way to Montreal to see his ailing mother and had spent the night in the railway shim-shack, which had a small coal-burning stove, but no coal left in the fender, back on the Rock Cut, a short distance from home. He said that he intended to catch the next freight train when it slowed down to make the upgrade. Papa, who as a young man had travelled the boxcar circuit, understood all of this and nodded in agreement with the old man's words.

Mamma set a plate for him at our breakfast table where there was a hearty serving of pancakes with overflowing molasses, homemade bread, and baked beans chased down with the strong black tea. The old man ate like he had not tasted a bite in weeks – well, perhaps he hadn't. While, like Papa, I had an interest in the plight of our morning guest, Mamma never spoke to the man, remaining a country woman, retiring and a bit unsocial, the aversion to strangers, especially railway tramps, occupying a good part of her nature.

Papa said, "Glad to have someone for a meal. We don't see many people out this way."

The old man did not seem to have a single point in common with Papa, yet in the current circumstance, they had become immediate friends with seemingly a sense of trust between them as I suppose his survival was in question. Perhaps the railway experiences had brought them together.

After breakfast, while the old man sat in the kitchen rocker and smoked a cigarette, my father mended his boots by hammering rivets through the souls on an anvil and Mamma found some good warm socks, a flannel shirt, and woolen gloves. After more tea and another cigarette, seeing our open piano in the dark wainscotted parlour, he sat down at the keyboard and played a wonderful old-time air, a seasonal classic which none of us knew the name of – we were not exactly of the violin classes – but had heard before on the radio.

As he played, his expressions changed from grimace to glee to despondency. And for a brief moment I pictured him as a young man with a dream of playing piano in some big concert hall, perhaps in Montreal or Boston, and that maybe he had not been able to turn this illusion into reality. I also thought that maybe there was a little bit of home and motherhood in the melody for him, the feelings of old times and a happy boyhood brought to his soul through the art of music. Or maybe it was self-love for the talented person he used to be, a man who had a dream but never got the breaks, and that he was probably lazy in everything but his art, as many artists are, and had put all of his hopes on that happening. And that was why he was so poor.

But on this dismal winter morning, the music brought me a feeling that was as soul-warming as the summer sun and in which appeared intonations of my grandfather, a man who was long dead but was said to have once been a bagman for a time. Sometimes a man will risk something solid in order to find notoriety, I thought. And perhaps that had been where my grandpapa's dream, and downfall, had come from: the fear of what could happen in life from just one bad decision.

I tried to divine the depth of this man's inner life and if he still had a dream of better things to come, even now at his age. Perhaps this little visit was an escape for him on such a dismal morning, having awakened to find himself cold, in a railway shack from where he headed out looking for the window light where someone might take him in, help him get a new start, keep the fading dream alive until he could swing it all around. And I felt that he was probably not anywhere near being as old as he looked, the hard life having aged him to biblical proportions.

Having experienced the morning's events, I felt changes within myself. I knew I would never be able to take home and family for granted again. And I would find no peace of mind until I was sure this old man had found his ailing mother and family. I could remember seeing poorly clothed people sleeping in alleys when I went to town with Mamma and Papa. And I felt that in town, people do not help one another as country people do. Those beggars all had the same look of defeat in their eyes. Well, they *were* defeated after following a dream that I suspect was beyond reach, or perhaps no dream at all. And I thought that maybe they had not taken life seriously when they were young, having lived one day at a time for the simple amusement there was in it. "Ingenuity be damned, why not go for all or nothing?" they might have said. "Why not gamble a bit of real life on a dream?"

The old man got up from the piano and prepared to leave, though I could read in his eyes that he did not really want to go. He reached into his little packsack and brought out a small Indigenous arrowhead, perfect in proportion, a flint stone among millions that he had probably picked up on the railway. He passed it to me saying, "Sanny Claus gave this ta me ta give ta you." (That little flint arrowhead was authentic and I still have it in my top bedroom drawer.) We all bid the old man goodbye and he was gone on his way back down the lane, with a musical stride, through the projecting corn-stubble, the wintery trees, on toward the gray railroad gate from where he would hobble along toward the Rock Cut so he could climb aboard that slow-moving freight train.

"The very best of a lad," Papa said.

The morning visitor reminded me of a time one summer when a First Nation elder from the Esgenoôpetitj Reserve near Burnt Church came to our place in the early morning because he wanted to get a fresh start. He was in search of ash trees because he wanted to make baskets to sell at the big Powwow that was to follow in Prince Edward Island. He had also slept on a bench in that railway shack. Papa sharpened his axe on the grindstone and then took him back into our woods to a place called Weasel Brook and showed him a dozen ash trees – all ash belong to the First Nations' people, he said – and the old man went to work chopping and beating. But after a few days he gave it up and went back to the Reserve. The fallen trees were left to rot. I can remember seeing them in the woods years later when I was a teen, hunting with my father. "Why don't we take them for stove wood?" I asked.

"Those trees are not our property! They belong to the Indians," he said.

But now it was a time to secretly wonder if our morning guest had made it home to Montreal. And like my father, I dreamed of him often, in my case, in the past tense. (Maybe it was out of the fear that every man has of ending up in a similar predicament.) But dreams have a short memory and soon reality will replace their spiritual revelations. Like youth and old loves, they are never to be recaptured. The old man has faded from my conscious life, except when I am in my bedroom and in the top bureau drawer I stumble upon a little Indigenous arrowhead that Santa Claus sent to me.

It was a few weeks later, on toward Christmas, that we read in the newspaper that the old man had been an armed robber and a killer, that he had been picked up by railway detectives and taken back to prison.

A Winter Wood

It is early December and I have found work as a greeter at Walmart in the Regent Mall. Like many senior citizens who need money, I work evenings, from four until midnight. It is a clean job where I can dress up in a white shirt, red company vest, and black trousers, to stand in the entrance, away from the cold wind and snow that drifts across the parking lot and dances in a frenzy under the lights. This is not a fit evening to be out of doors, I think. But here inside the mall there is seasonal music being played throughout and because I am deprived socially, I enjoy meeting the many friendly people who come to shop. "Welcome," I say. "Come in! Happy Holidays!"

My mother, who has lived with me in Fredericton for the past fifteen years, is now in a seniors' home, where I visit her daily and we reminisce about former times when we lived on our farm in the northeast of the province. Sometimes my sisters, Becky and Janet, join us and the conversation that goes on through the afternoons brings back that old way of life, as vivid as if we are watching a home video.

In that old day, right after Thanksgiving, the fishing season closed for the year and the sport anglers went back to their comfortable city homes, leaving the river – it had become a forlorn bed of moving tar – with an abundance of spawning salmon. Upon black gravel, black water whispered in a gait of spooky, yet contented freedom, between the rocky shoals and the tall shore grasses that were by then orange and, from the river breezes, jangling like the tails of rattlesnakes. The remaining leaves having blown from the bank trees to submerge and drift away, there was a desolate bareness about the black birch and leafless poplar. The blue hills in the distance edified the pall of smoke from farmhouse kitchens, a scented haze that revealed to neighbours what kind of firewood each had gathered. The songbirds have gone south and the scent from chimneys attracted the lowly Canada jay. Those beautiful wintery birds alighted on the floors of our open verandas and gathered the bread crumbs that we scattered for them, to be carried away and hidden in the branches of pasture trees.

Each year, after the river closed, in those gray but dry days of late October, my father and I plowed the river intervale, turning the cow-manure-speckled sod upside down from the line to garden fence, one crumbling furrow at a time. The harness squeaked and the chains jingled as Papa closed one eye and sighted between the horse's ears to make the furrows straight, his big hands clamping the plow handles as though he were wrestling a bull. He stumbled to keep the disc-coulter cutting the same depth, while the mouldboards hove the arrow-straight furrows to lie on their backs as we turned the flat into a corduroy plain of chocolate loam. It was the biggest field that I could remember plowing with one horse and I was almost fifteen years old. (As was the custom for the oldest son, I had quit school in grade nine to help my aging father keep the farm going, raise and educate my sisters.) All other fall chores had been done: the vegetables put in their cellar bins, the house banked with fir boughs, snow fences erected, and the machinery put into sheds before the big rains came. By this time with the ground having frozen, we were expecting snow any night.

As the days grew shorter and darker and our clocks were set back, the fading sun, which had no heat left in it, peeked over the distant horizon in horizontal, frost-flaked beams. It was like the projector's shaft of light we used to see in the old movie house in Stanton. For an instant I thought that with our long shadows that danced before us, we were storybook giants in a horror film. The scattered field ponds were now frozen into sheets of stained glass, the plowed land was a corduroy plain that was surrounded by orange sod. The big northeast rains had swept up the valley for days, blowing needle-like squalls against our storm windows and outside doors. It painted our cedar-shingled barn, where our cattle and horses were stalled, a tombstone black.

Papa, because of hard work at home in his youth, a stint overseas from 1944 to '45, and a smoking habit, was old for his years. As we raked the last of our elm leaves from the yard, he used a red pocket handkerchief to wipe his leaking nose. He had a rasping cough that forced him to bend over and spit into the rain-washed grass.

With the farm work done, Papa and I laboured on our woodlot. Bundling up in our pitch-scented mackinaw coats, with wide suspenders holding up our wool trousers and our gum rubbers laced to the top, we left our wood-fired kitchen range in the darkness of the early mornings to walk across that rocky hillside beyond the railway and over a mile into the woods. At such hours Mamma was busy making lunches for my sisters' school day. Becky, who was eight years old, was in grade two and Janet, who was twelve, was in the sixth grade. They walked down the road to the one-room Thornton School, which was on a hill overlooking the big river with its waves that rolled against the rocks to make a creamy foam when the north wind blew. As Papa and I journeyed into the still-darkened woods – it was always darker under the trees – we followed the horse along the deep-rutted, partly grown-over truck roads that had purple patches of broken ice and a tangle of black alders that slapped our pant legs like horse-whips in the hands of angry bosses. As we walked, Papa, always happy in the morning, always happy in the woods, sang an old song from his youth.

At this time of year, there seemed to be a sense of warmth in the woods, the trees offering us a kind of shelter from the bare and lifeless fields, those upriver, northeast winds. Still, I wondered why Papa was so content to work the long days in the bush for so little money, and not reach higher – get a job in town where he could dress in a suit and tie and work the shorter day, free of the elements. But like his father and grandfathers for five generations before him, this was his life and he dreamed for nothing more; the trees were companions that helped maintain the standard of living we enjoyed. And I knew this way of life was also my destiny.

"Allen is a great boy to work," I overheard Papa say to Mamma one evening. "He's strong in the arms."

Papa's way of thinking was not in agreement with my mother's. Mamma was a meticulous reader and when we were children, she read to us in the evenings – especially at Christmastime – long passages from the works of George Eliot and Charles Dickens. "A novel is a mirror journeying down the high road, reflecting the azure blue of heaven," she had said. In some ways she was like Papa in that she was not happy unless she was busy, always driving forward, though perhaps in the opposite direction than his, which I suppose brought a sense of balance to our household. She scolded me for quitting school, saying that I had potential to do great things, so why would I settle for woods-work as a career. "It's the kind of job that will keep you poor and make you old before your time," she said.

I was caught between Mamma's philosophy and Papa's more practical view of things. Mamma had come here with Papa – she was fifteen years younger – as a war bride from Devon, England, and I knew she felt buried on this small farm. She would never adapt. According to old wartime photographs, Mamma standing beside Papa in uniform, she had been a handsome woman: tall with high cheekbones and black hair that fell upon her bulging breasts. Her moistened eyes were large and blue, so filled with love and tenderness they would attract attention in a crowded room. While she never liked the ruggedness of our country, the lack of culture, and grieved the loss of her old homeland, she was loyal to my father. After almost twenty years in Canada, she still spoke with an English accent.

My sisters were reincarnations of our mother and had Mamma's striking eyes. Whatever they did became an art. Anyone could see that when these young women matured, they would also have class. They took piano lessons from Mamma, and Janet could play John Field's *Concerto No. 1 in E Flat Major*, as well as Beethoven's *Sonata No. 2 in C Sharp Minor*. Janet would go over and over a passage and Mamma would say to her, "Almost but not quite. You have to put more soul into it. Now let's take it from the top." My sister, correcting her timing, would put a tender refrain into the piece, especially Beethoven's *Moonlight Sonata* that always brought me to tears. Sitting in a wicker chair on the veranda, with eyes closed, from where I could hear these pieces being played so many times, every pure note became familiar to my ears. How like her mother, I thought. Mamma sometimes played Tosti's *Ave Maria* or Handel's *Largo* and the loving voice of the piano always aroused pleasant thoughts in my ears in an otherwise tuneless community. I still remember those fine pieces of music being played by Janet with flaws, and then without flaws.

At Christmastime, I went with Mamma and Papa down the road to my sisters' school concerts where, wearing new dresses and new shoes, they did recitations and songs. Sometimes, as a family, we drove our pea-green '55 Pontiac to the nearby village of Stanton where we attended a church service. To this, Mamma wore her blue suit and pillbox hat that had a veil, and Papa was in his white shirt and religious-bent Orangeman's necktie. In church we found comfort as we prayed to God in Heaven. After the service we visited the graves of Grandmother, Grandfather, Great-grandmother and Great-grandfather, members of our family I had never met, but whom I had pictured in my mind as poorly carved versions of Papa. On these trips to the village, Papa always drove the car in the middle of the gravel road, a habit from his days as a teamster and which was dangerous on blind hills.

"This is a good life," Papa told me many times. "Where would we go to find more freedom? Where would we find better neighbours? How could we get any closer to the land that keeps us clothed and eating well?"

Like the horse, Papa moved among the trees as if he were an old woods' spirit. No longer with the stamina of his early years, it was like he was a generations-old relative to the spruce and pine trees that stood around us and which supplied us with our livelihood, but hid us from the sun. In the tree-shaded woods one sees less but feels more, I thought. In a stand of white pine near Morse Brook, we found our power-saw and axes. And even though it was a cold morning and the bracken was white with frost, we threw our coats onto the ground and set out to work the long day, sawing and chopping until it was almost dark. Papa kneeled down in the moss and, with his sharp axe, undercut the big trees to make them shiver and drop needles and snow that melted under our coat collars while sending the sap-moistened chips to scatter in the brakes. He did this with little effort as if it came as a second nature to him.

I would hold down on the throttle and crank the chainsaw, which was a thirty-pound Lombard that had a clutch. It started to hum and then it revved up in a blue cloud of smoke and a strong smell of gasoline. And even now so many years later, I can still hear the whining of the saw as it laboured through the pitch-scented tree trunks and sprayed yellow sawdust onto the legs of my trousers and into my boots. The sound carried a long way on those hollow days before a storm. And I remember it thus, from a distance, in the crisp autumn air, fading away as a dream fades. When the tree fell, with a great crashing sound, Papa uses his axe to chop off the limbs, while I set out to saw the tree into twelve- and fourteen-foot logs. Sometimes we counted the rings on a stump to see how old a tree was, how fast it had grown.

. Through the day, we stopped only long enough to eat two lunches, smoke a cigarette, and file the saw after brewing tea over a pitch-wood fire. As Papa drank his tea abstractly, the flames lit up his face like a copper coin. These lunch breaks divided the workday into threes. Because we were wet with sweat, we put on our coats at lunchtime. We sat on our pitch-coated leather mittens so that we would not get a cold in our butts or develop piles. And we tossed our crumbs to the moose birds that glided into the lunch hole, canted their white heads, and looked at us with their dark, bead-like eyes. With me running the saw and Papa doing the axe work, each day we cut down thirty tall pine trees to get seventy-five twelve- and fourteen-foot logs, to be skidded upon the yards with a piling chain and eventually rolled onto the forks of iron log-loaders and lifted to the boxes of the three-ton GMC or Ford trucks, to be chained there and taken to the sawmill in town.

In the dusk of wintertime, we hid our working implements in the brush and headed out the same trail, the frost-whiskered horse leading us back to her warm stall and our warmer kitchen that smelled of a beef and vegetable stew, pickles in the making, and the sour smell of the washstand where the half-filled pails of water stood, the teakettle singing on the stove. As I filled the wood-boxes for the night, Papa went first to the barn where he took the harness off the mare before feeding her, along with the cows and hens. Before he came into the kitchen, he swept the snow off his boots with a straw broom. The wind slammed the storm door behind him and snow sifted in onto the kitchen floor, the nails in the door white from the frost. Because of the smell of horse on his coat, Papa hung it on a nail on the inside of the outside door. "Boys, she's a cold old night out there," he said. "Freeze the balls off a brass monkey."

I had not told Papa or Mamma about this, but when I was in Bradford the summer before, I applied for a job in a few department stores. These would be clean places to work, I thought, free of the cold, the snow and rain that Papa and I worked through in the fall as we pushed for Christmas money. We also had to keep the family clothed and eating well through the winter after the snow got too deep for woods' work, although we had raised our own vegetables, pork, and beef and Mamma had knit wool socks and mittens for everyone. In the woods in the rain under the sweat-steaming clothes, we became soaked and our coats and flannel shirts stuck to our backs, our leather mittens becoming useless rags that no longer protected our hands from blistering. We wrung the water from them by twisting them into knots and then we hung them by the fire. This was also the case when it was snowing and the heavy flakes stuck to our wool coats to make them white and steamy, eventually soaking us to the skin.

At suppertime, with the scraping of hardwood chairs, we sat in our accustomed places at the kitchen table, with Papa near the pantry on one end and Mamma on the other, her head bowed to say grace. One evening during supper, Mamma told me that Stedmans Department Store in Bradford had phoned our house and that they had a job opening and would like me to come in for an interview as soon as possible. This excited me, and for a brief moment I had an image of myself in dress clothes, a new car of my own, an apartment in town. But right away I could see the disappointment on my father's face even though he did not say anything, one way or the other. I believed he was too old to work in the woods alone by then, and had been counting on my being there with him as he had been with his father, and before that, his father with his father.

Mamma said, "You have those gray pants and white shirt you got for Linda's wedding last June, and you have your father's fine shoes that will now fit you." She flashed a preoccupied, sad smile.

Janet said, "Allen is moving up in the world. He's going to be a businessman!"

"You'll become a town sissy!" Becky said, tugging my hair.

"Maybe he'll become a Fuller Brush or a Picture Bible salesman."

Sensing Papa's concern about my mission in town, I felt like I was a traitor and was embarrassed that I had done this thing behind his back, without talking it over with him. He did not finish his supper. Instead he got up from the table and went into the parlour where he sat in the rocking chair and smoked his pipe, his faded blue eyes staring at the opposite wall. I thought, it is not an easy thing to back away from a lifestyle that has been in the family for so many generations. And it is a harder go still to move on and leave your fast-aging father to work in the woods alone and try to support the little ones that have been counting on Papa and me. And I wondered if my father would have done something like this to his father, but guessed not, as these were agreements between fathers and oldest sons that were not much spoken about, rather understood.

"Papa, I'm sorry, I should have told you before," I stammered. "But I can bring home some money if I work my way up in that company that has many branches."

"I guess I knew this day would come," he said without taking his eyes from the wallpaper across the room. "I won't hold ya back. I wish ya luck in town. But it's a thing that I could never do meself. I wouldn't like that kind of work." He did not look at me. More resolutely he kept staring at the flowers on the wall.

"I may not get that job a-tall," I said to soften his anxiety. But job or no job, I knew the damage had already been done.

Later, when I went upstairs to my bedroom, I could see that Mamma had already laid my dress clothes across the bed. Father's brown shoes were placed upon a chair along with Janet's white ankle socks, one of which was worn through at the heel. These stockings were too small but were all the dress socks that I had. I said my prayers and got into bed where I stared at the ceiling, seeing my father's disappointed face in the whitewashed plaster. The clock ticked loudly as the hours crawled by, leaving me in a state of unrest and shame. Through the night, from across the hall I could hear my father's rasping cough, his spitting into a chamber pot, the scent of tobacco smoke. Because of his night-smoking and coughing, by then my mother was sleeping in the spare room down the hall.

In the morning, I dressed in the wedding clothes, Janet's socks, Papa's shoes, and Grandfather's necktie which was flowered and out of style. Though feeling guilty for eating at home now, perhaps this one last time, I had a good breakfast of buckwheat porridge and went out to stand on the roadside to wait for the bus. At the table there had been no conversation, Papa having gotten up quickly to go and feed the horse. I heard his coughing in the barn as I stood by the roadside. In my right hand I had the pork sandwich and apple that Mamma had put into a plastic bag for me. I could see her briefly as she stood in the front porch, a dish towel in her hand. My sisters had come outside to watch the bus arrive.

On the chip-seal road, I paced, back and forth, back and forth, as I was still not sure as what I should do. Finally, I could see the bus, with its many bright cab lights and marquis that read "Bradford" coming around the far bend and my pace quickened as if there was a solid decision that would come from this exercise. But of course there was no right decision. All of our lives, the little ones included, had been thrown into a state of uneasiness with the news of my taking a job in town and perhaps leaving home.

At last the big bus pulled up in front of me, the double-hinged doors squeaked open and, having gotten a hug from Becky and Janet, I climbed up the steps to pay the uniformed driver and make my way to the back seat where I would be alone to think things out on the hour-long ride to town. As the bus pulled away from our front gate, I looked out through the hazy back window to see Mamma waving her towel from the porch. And my sisters ran after the bus for a few yards. Papa and the horse were going across the highway, heading back the old woods' road for another long day of logging. He was hunchbacked that morning, like a deer that had been wounded but still standing. Strong men suffer in silence, I thought.

Along the way, school children walking along the roadside waved good-naturedly as the bus passed them. There were neat houses and barns, their dooryards raked clean by the fall winds and rain, washed and neat like our own yard, their brown expanse of plowed fields and purple meadows awaiting the snow. On one such farm a dozen sheep huddled in the lee of two gray sheds. With the slanting and crooked buildings and the humble farm animals, it looked like a Bible scene. We stopped only twice to pick up passengers, and once at a railroad crossing where the driver opened the double-hinged door before moving on.

Soon, the town of Bradford stood before me with its clapboard, false-fronted stores that were squeezed together along Castle Street. These buildings, with their roosting pigeons, were blistered from the rugged winds that swept up the big river from where the crashing surf pounded the ledged shores of Northumberland Strait, the white seagulls screaming in busy flocks. And there was the honk of car horns, the scream of police sirens, hiss of air brakes from the buses, and the scent of burnt diesel fuel. In the upstairs windows, where I assumed the apartments were, there were geraniums still in bloom. I was filled with excited wonder. And I thought, it is good to be in town for whatever reason. It is good to be away from the old routine for a while. I found Stedmans, which, according to the bus driver, was on Queen's Square.

I went inside to look for the manager. The store was big and brightly lit and there were a hundred smells, all of which were artificial, like chemicals and water paints and the plastic gadgets we find in children's stockings at Christmastime. Chamber music was playing softly and from the lamps, the tile floor had a pink shine, like a sunrise on the March crust of snow. The overhead lights were also bright and dazzling. For sure there is no snow or tree spills to fall down one's neck in here, I thought. And for a brief moment an image of Papa came to me. He was stooped over and cranking the power-saw, an implement that he was not exactly sure how to operate as I had always done the sawing. But then, as a clerk in a red vest approached me, my father was gone from my mind. I asked the employee where the manager's office was and she pointed to a corner cubicle that was up three steps and had a window overlooking the sales floor. When I knocked on the office door someone shouted, "Come in, Allen!" And I guessed that he could tell by the way I was dressed that I was the lad from upriver he was waiting to see. Even now, so many years later, I blush at the memory of that experience.

The store manager's name was Cecil McDonald. He was a tall, slim, well-dressed young man who told me that he originated from Cape Breton, Nova Scotia, and that he got into the store business himself to escape the sea and the coal mines. He asked many questions about my background and my education, of woods' work, farming, and river guiding and he told me that he had an opening for a manager trainee. "It's an occupation where, after six months of on-the-job-training, the new employee will take over this or another store in a bigger centre," he said.

I felt it had been a good interview and I liked Mr. McDonald, who seemed to have honest eyes. He shook my hand and told me that he would call me in a few days after he had interviewed more people. When I asked him what he thought my chances were of getting the job, he told me that he had interviewed twelve people so far and had narrowed it down to four applicants and that I was one of the four. This made me feel good and I shook hands with him and walked out of the store and down the street to Jean's Restaurant, loosening my tie as I went. In the restaurant I sat in a booth and ordered a coffee to go with the sandwich and apple that Mamma has packed for me. I was a bit self-conscious, but to tell the truth, I was really excited about just hanging out in a diner, sipping coffee, and listening to the town conversations about playing bridge and the game of curling.

I walked around town many times as I tried to find the pulse of the urban life. I smiled and spoke to girls on the sidewalk but most did not respond. They are not like country people, I thought. Why speak to a stranger like me? None of these young women were the one of my dreams, the one who was a part of three different women I had had a crush on but still had never found, the way that dreams go. So I went to the big terminal, played the jukebox, read *Teen Magazine*, and waited for the upriver bus to leave. In the autumn twilight, the drive home was boring, but filled with a new-found sense of possible progress and acceptance.

When I got to our house, even though it was dark outside, Papa was not yet home from the woods. Mamma and the girls were worried that maybe he had gotten lost. I was worried too as I knew how punctual he was about the working hours, both his and the horse's. I changed into my work clothes and headed back the dark woods road toward where we had been working. After being in the warm bus, I found the autumn air to be cold and crisp. Into the woods a short distance, I met Papa coming. With bent knees, he was stumbling behind the horse and looking very tired. I asked how many logs he had cut and he told me that he could not remember. "It takes longer when you're alone," he said without stopping. He did not ask how my interview went in town. And I thought, I have to work things out with Papa.

Later in the evening, I phoned Stedmans and told Mr. McDonald that I would not be taking the job and for him to scratch me off the list. "I am more needed here at home where I am expected to help to keep things running," I told him. "My father needs me more than the Stedmans Company does right now, I guess." I said these words with reluctance as I could see a job in store management slipping away, the white-collar escape being my one chance to better myself. I knew I would have to stay here as long as my father was alive. But I also had a feeling of pride for having, so quickly, made the decision to support my family. And I could sense a rekindled comfort in the ones around me, even though I could see that Mamma was not pleased. For a time she stayed in her bedroom, the door locked.

"Intellect is always independent of the heart," McDonald said. "Home is more than just a place. But let me know if you change your mind." And I knew that he had chosen me for the manager trainee program.

Restraining all thoughts of town and my long-term future, before daylight, the next morning, I went back to the woods with Papa, singing now as he walked. The trees stood ghostly against a dull sky, seeming to be content with my return. And during those hollow November days before the coming of the snow, which would muffle the sounds, the whines and howls of the power-saw could be heard for a long way through that wood. It seemed to echo along the brook for miles. Because of my success in town, my spirits were lifted and I was riding high with confidence. It is always good to have an option, I thought. Papa appeared to be doing things to appease me, patronizing like. As if he was afraid that I would walk away from my responsibilities again. "Are you tired, Allen?" he would say. "Let's take a break, have a smoke." And we would sit together on a log and smoke his tailor-made cigarettes.

On the eighteenth of December, we sold our logs to the sawmill in Stanton and Papa gave me eighty-five dollars, which I hid in my closet. Fearing I would be left behind when my parents were gone, I would need this money to get me away from what could become a desolate countryside – away out of Thornton, out of Falconer County, out of the Province of New Brunswick forever. Although I had not told these secret plans to my parents or to my sisters.

Later, most of this money was used to pay the doctor when Janet fell ill with pneumonia.

Through the years that followed, Papa and I carried on with the centuries-old routine and had no thought whatsoever of either of us wanting to do anything more than to farm, guide, and lumber. We worked the long hot days of summer, slapping mosquitoes while bringing in the hay. We guided on the shimmering summer water for weeks at a time – we were looking for salmon that were, by this time, fewer – harvested the grain, plowed our fields in the late fall, and worked the cold bitter days in the winter wood. I walked in the fields alone in the peaceful calm of Sunday mornings, my one free day from the woods. I was contemplating old longings that I felt would never see fruition. I wondered where my future would lead me.

As Papa and I laboured through the lavender sunrises that turned the snow to scarlet, the green sunsets that set the treetops aflame, I watched as my sisters grew into pretty young women. Almost without me noticing, they had gone from walking with their friends to the little one-room school with a lunch pail and book bag on their arms to climbing aboard the big yellow buses that took them to the high school in town, to the graduation ceremonies Mamma and I attended, with tears in our eyes. They grew into very proud and beautiful young adults, like my mother would have been in her youth, with their tall demeanour and long black hair that fell upon their developing breasts. And I envied them.

One after the other they moved to the city, first to the university and then to good-paying jobs in Fredericton's big office buildings. At first they came home to visit on weekends and then later they did not come home except at Easter, Thanksgiving, and Christmas. They brought with them their business-minded boyfriends, tall, good-looking young men with soft hands that displayed expensive university rings and well-manicured nails. These men seemed to know nothing about the river, the land, and the trees that had kept my family eating and clothed through so many generations. And my sisters did not mention these humble things to them and appeared to be embarrassed by the downtrodden road they had come. Later they brought home their children to whom I had become the tobacco-smelling bachelor uncle.

As Papa watched his daughters grow away from him, move on to more educated ways, educated people, he and I were still spending the winter hours in the woods, in all weather. By then, though, we were working a shorter day. Papa was in his early eighties and badly used up with rheumatism from kneeling on the frozen ground, and the ruptures he had gotten from lifting timber onto the log yards we had so often built on the roadside – more wood to be trucked to the sawmill. In his autumnal decline, Papa had become a frail old man, his shoulders hunched, his big nose leaking, and with a curve along his spine, his lungs congested from his many years of smoking tobacco. By this time, Papa was wearing a rubber girdle to keep his abdomen in place as well as a jock strap that supported his testicles. His knees had also given out from all the kneeling into the frozen roots to chop the undercuts, for it was he and he alone who could do this job properly. Despite the wind, he could prevent those long red pines from lodging in the branches of other trees that were not quite as big, thus separating this day's working harvest from tomorrow's.

I can still smell the pitch, the sap, the sawdust, and the gasoline in the saw. Papa was known in the community for being a keen axe-man and he was proud of this trait. But I was at the point where I worried about him constantly, thinking perhaps he might fall on his axe. And there were mornings when I would say to him, "Papa, it's raining out. Papa, it is snowing. Why don't we take the day off? Why don't we stay home from the woods today? We have enough logs cut now, enough money earned to get us through the winter."

"Well, let's go back for a little while anyway," he would say. "There are only a few snow flurries drifting around. The Hennessey and the Keenan men are working today. I could hear their chainsaws when I went out to feed the horse. And let's leave the house early so we're not seen going to work in the late morning or perhaps not at all, like town people or schoolteachers do because it's raining or snowing out."

And I believed, I always believed, that Papa would work in the woods until he collapsed. Because men like my father did not know the meaning of the word *retirement*. They did not know the meaning of what it would be like to stay at home on a bad day, sit by a cosy fire and read *Great Expectations*. While occasionally I read from Mamma's small collections of Dickens, Hardy, Austen, and George

Eliot, Papa had no time for books. He had no time for higher educated people and the frivolous things that had taken his daughters away to the city, never to return. Also, the other woodsmen, his peers, would think it strange that he had stopped lumbering because of foul weather. Was he sick? Was he injured? So we worked the regular hours, in all conditions, even though by this time Papa was capable of doing less and less each day. In the process of twitching the logs to the road, he stumbled behind the horse like a hunched-over ghost that had been dressed in a diaper, a mackinaw coat, and felt hat. And he coughed from the constant cigarette that stood between his nicotine-stained teeth.

Each day, at the lunch hole, to ward off the cold winter air, we put on our coats, sat with our elbows on our knees by a pitch-wood fire to eat our molasses-sweetened pork sandwiches, and drank the thick-tasting black tea we always brewed in a tin pail. Afterwards Papa would take a walk to cruise out a chance for the afternoon's cutting and also to go to the john, which was a hollow log that he sat upon to relieve his bloodied and painful bowels. And I would wait for him – with that smell of pitch in my brain, pine smoke drifting through the trees, and the death bells jangling in my ears – to come back to the fire-site. And I was always relieved when this happened.

Until one day in December when he didn't return, and there was a great unrest with the crows and also with the stomping, whinnied horse that would later be driven by a Stanton RCMP officer as he pulled Papa's remains out of the woods on a portage shed. I went to look for him. It was there, sitting on the hollow log in that stooped-over position, not a hundred yards from where we had been lunching, that I found my father. His felt hat had fallen from his head, there was sawdust and pine needles in his hair that was white as cotton, his wool coat still warm and damp with sweat from the morning's labour. His faded blue eyes were open as if he were staring at the dreary winter snow which had become mixed with his warm blood, urine, and excrement to make it a dirty slush that melted into the roots, as Papa's soul and body became a bigger part of that wood. It was as if he had foreseen his death coming and wanted it to happen there among the trees that he loved.

Feeling like I was going to faint, I grabbed the limb of a pine tree for support, a tree that seemed to realize that I could use a helping hand just then. Papa had obviously collapsed, having hemorrhaged to death before he even realized what was happening. I believe this to be the case because I could have heard him shout from where I was sitting by the fire.

And instantly I knew that his long years of woods' work, too often in the worst of conditions, his great pride in having done an honest day's labour, always lifting above his weight – for he was famous among his peers for this – had overtaken him finally, and that he was gone from this earth forever. It took a while for me to realize all this, so that I could cry for him, alone there, among the sighing, whispering trees that stood around me and were such a big part of us both.

* * *

For a few years after Papa's death, on fall days of wind, rain, and snow, Mamma and I sat by the fire in our farmhouse parlour and we read. The clock ticked slowly in the autumn evenings and the days appeared longer, time being measured by the books we exchanged, the voices within. I could never return to that wood, which had become filled with the ghosts not only of Papa, but also of his father and his father before him. And my own young ghost too, because I could see myself drifting into that old dogmatic mindset. And I think that dreams are empty things unless they are backed up by willpower. In the words of Marcel Proust, *"Only the one who makes a promise can feel guilty for the way things come down."* It is not an easy thing to come to terms with one's own ghost.

Maintaining the horse until she died of old age, we had let the farmlands grow up into poplar and birch, the talk of idle countrymen. And the great river where Papa and I had spent so many days working the boats in search of Atlantic salmon had become a forgotten dream, an entity that was never spoken about. We waited for the real estate people to come and evaluate the wood property, the farmlands, and the fishing rights, with the thought of selling it all if the money was right, as that old way of life as we knew it had died forever and would become nothing more than a memory that would wash away in the wheel ruts of the big tree farmers that would come to do a winter's work, in any conditions, in just a few days.

The yellow, double-hinged Caterpillar tractors, the big orange Cat harvesters with the wheels ten feet high, the long flat-bedded trucks with a hundred chains and higher stakes, and the long-arm hydraulic lifts came, not only to take the ghosts out of our woods, but also to take the woods itself, the trees, the spirit, and indeed its healing power for those of us who had lived there and loved it. (Ruptures and sprains be damned, how do you embrace something for so many generations and not love it?) They left an open plain, to be replanted with saplings in the new industrial way of tree harvesting, rugged hectares of chewed-up and shredded undergrowth, a snarl of treetops, and jagged stumps.

I felt guilty for letting this happen as I cherished the trees as family, like my father did. But I knew too that by then, it had become a new day, with a more modern electronic way of thinking, of making a living. The so-called jackknife operation, like Papa and I had been contented with – old black and white photographs of log cutters standing together on the wall, to be admired – had disappeared forever and farming in the old-fashioned sense, guiding for salmon that were no longer in the river, and the select-cutting of trees to be hauled to the road with an aging horse was a way of life that had gone forever from our river and others like it.

When we are in our youths, the powers of the mind are directed solely toward the not-too-distant future and those young dreams spur us into manhood and eventually old age. But like my father, I am contrary and still want to fulfill my lifelong ambition, realizing that at my age, the bigger dream of escaping out-of-province to find success, my secret aspirations to become a "somebody," can never fully be realized. Yes, I have taken a job as a "greeter" in a department store in the capital city, so that I can dress up in the afternoons, go to work in a warm place, have lunch at the counter without always having to combat the wind on the river, the washed-out harvest, the snow, sleet, and rain, the tree spills, the chips, and the yellow sawdust that fell into my tea and sprayed down under the collar of my wool coat, in that now empty world of winter.

Acknowledgements

I would like to thank my first readers, Carrol Nesbit, David Adams Richards, Cynthia Lozier, and Heather Browne as well as my editor, Julia Swan. I am also grateful to Dennis Duffy and the staff at Trabon Group of Kansas City for their design of leaflets and posters.

The story "River Love" appeared in the summer 21 edition of *The Fiddlehead Magazine*. "The Cains (A River of Broken Promise)" appeared in the fall edition (2019) of the *Atlantic Salmon Journal*. "Spring Waters" appeared in *Saltscapes*, Spring edition, 2020. "Sunshine and Water" appeared in the *Atlantic Salmon Journal*, Spring 2020. "River Places" appeared in 2020 in *The Antigonish Review*, No. 201-02. "War Bride" appeared in *The Dalhousie Review*, Fall 2021. "Our December Guest" appeared in *The Nashwaak Review*. Fall/Winter 2020/21 No. 44/45. "September Mourning" has been previously published in *The New Brunswick Reader*, September 6, 1999, and later in *River Stories* by Nimbus Publishing, 2020.

About the Author

Wayne Curtis was born in Keenan, New Brunswick, in 1943. He was educated at the local schoolhouse and St. Thomas University where he majored in English. He started writing prose when he was in grade school. His work has been described by *Books in Canada* as "A pleasure to read, for no detail escapes his discerning eye."

He has won the Richards Award for short fiction, The Lieutenant Governor's Award, and the CBC Drama Awards, as well as A and B grants from arts nb and The Canada Council. He has been a contributor to several newspapers, including *The National Post* and *The Globe and Mail*, as well as commercial magazines such as *Reader's Digest, Quill and Quire, Outdoor Canada, The Fly Fisherman* (USA), *Sporting Classics, Atlantic Insight*, and *The Atlantic Advocate*. Wayne's stories have also appeared in literary journals (*The Cormorant, The Fiddlehead, Pottersfield Portfolio, The Nashwaak Review, The Antigonish Review, The Dalhousie Review, The New Brunswick Reader*, and *New Maritimes*) and the anthologies *Atlantica, Country Roads, The STU Reader, Winter House, The Christmas Secret, Winter,* and *Down Home For Christmas*. His short stories have been dramatized on CBC Radio and CBC Television.

In the spring of 2005, Wayne Curtis received an Honorary Doctorate Degree (Letters) from St. Thomas University. In 2014, he was awarded the Order of New Brunswick and in 2018 the Senate Sesquicentennial Medal from the Canadian Senate.

Wayne has lived in southern Ontario, Yukon, and Cuba. He currently divides his time between the Miramichi River and Fredericton, New Brunswick. *River People* is his twentieth published book.

Books by Wayne Curtis

Currents in the Stream
One Indian Summer
Fishing the Miramichi
River Guides of the Miramichi
Preferred Lies
The Last Stand
River Stories
Green Lightning
Fly-Fishing the Miramichi
Monkeys in a Looking Glass
Wild Apples
Night Train to Havana
Long Ago and Far Away
Of Earthly and River Things
Sleigh Tracks in New Snow
In The Country
Homecoming
Fishing the High Country
Winter Road
River People